T0131784

The Stockton Saga 5

Stockton's Law

Steven Douglas Glover

iUniverse®

THE STOCKTON SAGA 5
STOCKTON'S LAW

iUniverse books may be ordered through booksellers or by contacting:

iUniverse
1663 Liberty Drive
Bloomington, IN 47403
www.iuniverse.com
1-800-Authors (1-800-288-4677)

ISBN: 978-1-5320-8555-0 (sc)
ISBN: 978-1-5320-8556-7 (e)

Print information available on the last page.

iUniverse rev. date: 10/11/2019

CONTENTS

PREFACE

The *Stockton Saga* began as a short story for a friend. Her positive response encouraged me to write yet another tale of adventure. As others read my stories of gunfighter Cole Stockton, suggestions were made to put them together as a novel. Thus, *The Stockton Saga: Dawn of the Gunfighter* was born. It chronicles his heritage and the elements that formed his mystique.

The stories of Cole Stockton, a man of strong moral character, are infinite. *The Stockton Saga 2: Star of Justice* followed, revealing Stockton's rise to Deputy U.S. Marshal as well as meeting his lady love, Laura Sumner. My bounty of narratives about this man of the law led to *The Stockton Saga 3: A Man to Reckon With*. It continues Cole's encounters in the Lower Colorado Territory during the last half of the 19th Century.

Next, I thought it time to highlight the women of the Old West. *The Stockton Saga 4: The Lady From Colorado* presents lady rancher Laura Sumner in several situations that reveal her strength of character. She encounters danger on several occasions, oversees wranglers as she works alongside them on her horse ranch, and fights for justice for her aging parents. U. S. Marshal Cole Stockton remains a principle character in the novel.

I try to portray the Old West as it actually was, lending authenticity to the stories. Historical characters have been researched. When I speak of certain weapons, pistol or rifle, they have been researched as well. Smallest details of life and times currency, fashion, food, furniture, and businesses, are each presented as they were in the latter half of the 19th Century.

Many of my friends and fans continually ask me when the next Stockton novel is going to be out. This novel, *The Stockton Saga 5:*

Stockton's Law, fulfills their requests for more Cole Stockton. Wherever he travels, U.S. Marshal Cole Stockton invokes law, order, and justice.

Continued appreciation goes to my dear friend, Monti Lynn Eastin, for the persona of Laura Sumner. Her support of my writing and continuous prompting me to publish them is genuinely appreciated.

Once again, immense gratitude is given to Gay Lynn Auld for her time and effort editing this manuscript. Her suggestions for expansion proved invaluable.

A special thanks to Linda Glover, without whose review, comments, and moral support this book would not have been published.

Special thanks to my dedicated fans who continue to read my books and keep asking for more.

"The Stockton Saga 5: Stockton's Law"

I humbly dedicate this book to my wonderful wife, who
has been the cornerstone of my support in both writing my
stories as well as accompanying me to all of my book signings.
You are wonderful to me, Etta Linda Pybus Glover.

And to a very wonderful friend, as well as my
most able fantastic editor, Gay Lynn Auld.

And to

The memory of my most favorite Author, Louis L'Amour
1908 - 1988

This one is for you.

CHAPTER ONE

"Judge Wilkerson Arrested"

The late middle-aged couple had just sat down to breakfast on a chilly Colorado, January morning when a rapid banging resounded at their front door. Marie Wilkerson rose from the table while addressing her husband, "Stay seated, Joshua, and enjoy your coffee. I'll see to the door."

Marie moved quickly down the short hallway to the parlor and peered quizzically out the frosted front windows of her home. Three Eastern-dressed men stood bundled in warm coats on her porch. She opened the door slightly to inquire their reason for visiting at such an early hour.

"Is Joshua Wilkerson here?" boomed a husky voice.

"Yes, he is. May I tell him who is calling?"

Without responding to Marie's question, the three men crowded roughly into the parlor. One man held the slightly gray-haired woman to the side while the other two men stormed into the kitchen. Revolvers drawn, they faced a bewildered Judge Joshua Bernard Wilkerson, his napkin still tucked in at the neck of his starched white shirt.

"What is the meaning of this abominable intrusion?" queried the judge.

The leader of the crass trio announced sternly, "Joshua B. Wilkerson, you are under arrest for conspiracy. By the authority of the United States Magistrate, Washington, D.C., I, Special Agent Grant Newsome, hereby serve you with papers revoking your Federal Judge appointment to the Colorado Circuit Court, and ordering your arrest. You will be held in the Denver Jail until such time as we can arrange transportation to trial. Do you understand? Get your coat and hat, Mr. Wilkerson."

Fearing to disobey to risk Marie's safety, Joshua did as told. Special Agent Newsome somewhat sneered his next directive, "Put your hands out in front of you!"

Again, the stunned Judge Wilkerson complied and a second agent handcuffed him. The Eastern lawmen led him out the door

and shamelessly paraded him down Main Street of Denver to the jail.

Onlookers stood along the streets watching the grim procession. Joshua Wilkerson for all his years as a Federal Judge was being treated roughly, and with high disrespect. They led him through the streets like a horrendous criminal. Even so, knowing his own innocence, he walked proudly, head held high, and looking straight ahead.

Tears filled her eyes as Marie Wilkerson stood on her porch watching the quartet disappear down the street. Her heart ached with the humiliation afforded her precious husband. "What could he have possibly done to deserve this treatment? What might I do to help him?" she thought.

Marie lowered her head and made her way back inside her house. She entered the kitchen to pour a cup of hot black coffee. She sat at the table, her head clasped in her hands. She prayed aloud, "Help me, Lord. Tell me what to do!"

A moment later, her mind cleared with a sense of resolve. "Yes! I must get word to United States Marshal Cole Stockton. He will know just what to do."

Marie Wilkerson bundled up in her warmest coat and scarf and hurried through the snow-lined streets to the telegraph office.

* *

The morning light was just peeking into the window of another home in the state of Colorado as the sleeping, blanket-covered figure began to stir. The figure slightly stretched and suddenly stopped. Her eyes popped open. There was slight movement under her blankets. Something cold and wet brushed against her bare leg.

Laura Sumner lifted the blankets and peered down into the depths of her bed. She smiled and reached down to grasp the furry little puppy and cuddle it to her breast.

"Little Lady," she said in a mock scolding, "I don't mind the cuddling up but please keep your cold little nose off me."

Laura giggled as the golden-haired puppy licked her cheek.

"O.K., I know. It's time for you to go outside and sniff around."

Laura eased out of bed, pulling on her heavy robe, woolen socks, and slippers. This was early January 1879 and there was a carpet of white all across the land. It was cold in the house. She would start a fire in the wood stove.

She took the puppy in her arms and quickly walked to the door. An icy breeze met her face as she opened the door to let the puppy out. She shivered a bit and held her arms around herself while she watched the puppy sniff out its morning business.

Within minutes, the furry little creature was back at the door, looking up at Laura and happily wagging its tail.

Laura led to the kitchen where she built a fire in the cast iron cook stove. She filled the coffee pot with cold water and ground up fresh coffee beans while the fire crackled to life and began to take the chill out of the air. The puppy followed her everywhere around the kitchen.

The rich aroma of coffee brewing filled the kitchen when Laura heard *clunking* sounds from the living room.

"Cole is up and building a fire in the fireplace," she thought to herself and smiled when his image filled her mind. Cole awakened to the aroma of rich dark coffee brewing every morning.

A few minutes later a fully dressed Cole Stockton stepped into the kitchen. He walked over to Laura, gently kissed her cheek, and then, looked down at the puppy, that boyish grin spreading across his face.

"I heard the scolding <u>Lady</u> and I think you have been named now," he chuckled to himself.

Laura thought for a second, and looked down at the pup. "Lady! Yes, that will be your name from now on."

* *

The room was dim in the Omaha, Nebraska office where five well-dressed men of *The Association* sat around the table. They smoked fine cigars and sipped the finest brandy while they unraveled their current plans to expand their interests in the young state of Colorado.

Previous plans to rid the Territory of U.S. Marshal Stockton had failed. Men had been sent to kill the lawman; however, each attempt had failed.

Today they discussed their new plan. They would start from the top of the heap this time. False documents were created, and accusations were filed with the U.S. Magistrate in Washington.

They had "investors" in high government who pressured the Justice Department to bring charges against Judge Joshua Wilkerson to the effect that he had conspired and organized a gang of known gunmen, deputizing them to instill fear among the citizens. Easterners would not be privy to the truth. Anyway, to many, the untamed West was of little consequence. The plan was working.

Judge Wilkerson was to be discredited, stripped of authority, arrested and held in his own jail. Wilkerson's appointed Marshals and Deputies would be stripped of their badges and authority and disbanded.

The Association would pressure the Governor to appoint their choices for lawmen, allowing them to move quickly to establish their hold throughout the young state. No one would stop them this time.

CHAPTER TWO

"An Urgent Message"

Laura and I had just finished another of her hearty breakfasts of sliced ham, eggs, fried potatoes, homemade biscuits, honey, and, of course, the best coffee in the West.

The tranquility of the moment was broken when an urgent knocking came at the front door.

I went to the door to find Jimmy Leggett, the telegraph runner dancing around the porch, hugging himself. It was icy cold out and I could tell by the look on his half-froze face that the message he bore was of extreme importance. No one in their right mind would ride for an hour in near freezing temperatures to deliver a routine message.

"What is it, Jimmy?" I knew that the kid read every message that he carried, so there was no need to pretend that he didn't.

"Marshal Stockton. Judge Wilkerson has been arrested and is locked up in his own jail. Some Eastern fellers, Special Deputies or something like that, from Washington, took him from his home early this morning and marched him to jail. The message is from Mrs. Wilkerson and she says that something is *dreadfully* wrong and they need your help something fierce."

I took the telegram from him. "Thank you, Jimmy. How about a cup of hot coffee and some breakfast? You look like you could use some warming up."

"Thank you, Marshal Stockton. I sure could use some hot coffee. Is that biscuits I smell? I love Miss Laura's biscuits. Is there honey to go with them?"

"Go on in to the kitchen, Jimmy. Laura will fix you right up."

I stepped inside and closed the door to read the telegram. Some Eastern feller with Eastern ideals of a lawman took the Judge into custody. Two of the Deputy U.S. Marshals in town that were appointed by the Judge had their badges taken from them and discharged. Something was definitely wrong here, and I was going to ride up there to Denver and find out just what the Hell was going on.

"Laura, come here a minute, will you?"

"Yes, Cole. What is it?"

"Judge Wilkerson is in some sort of trouble. I'm riding up there right away to find out what is going on. I'd like some extra biscuits and ham to take with me. I don't know how long I'll be gone, but don't worry. I'll be back as soon as I can."

Laura nodded her understanding with a worried look on her face.

Two hours later I stopped in town to see Sheriff J.C. Kincaid. Something didn't set right about this turn of events and a notion of strange happenings was nagging in the back of my brain. I asked J.C. to keep his eyes and ears open for anything out of the ordinary. Something big was about to go down. I didn't know what it was now, but I was going to find out all I could.

After speaking with J.C., I once again swung into the saddle and Warrior broke into a fast trot toward Denver. I would be up there within a couple of days.

* *

Joshua Wilkerson paced back and forth in the cold cell. He thought hard and long, but he still couldn't figure out what was happening.

The warrant was legal, of that he was sure, but why? What were the specific accusations against him? He was not informed of these.

He overheard the loud talk, and protests outside the cell block as two of HIS appointed Deputy U.S. Marshals were relieved of their badges and dismissed. He grew angry at the circumstances.

Joshua Wilkerson had studied each and every man's qualifications and reputation before appointing him to wear the badge. The Colorado Territory was a wild and untamed area, teeming with lawlessness before he came on the scene. He had handpicked his law force and they were cleaning out the spoilers and scavengers with swift justice.

The people of the territory could rest easier in their beds at night because of his actions. Now—what was happening, now? Would the territory revert back to lawlessness? Will there be night raiders like before? Who would protect the citizens and serve justice?

Suddenly, it came to him.

There was one U.S. Marshal on his force that he had not personally appointed. He had recommended his appointment, but the actual appointment had come from the Executive Branch in Washington D.C. itself.

This U.S. Marshal Stockton could not be dismissed by the Special Agent.

Furthermore, any Deputy appointed by Stockton could not be dismissed, except by the U.S. Marshal himself. There was hope, a slim chance, but a very promising chance.

Joshua Wilkerson leaned back in the sturdy cot, suddenly chuckled to himself, and a big grin spread across his face,

"I'd like to see them Eastern lawmen's faces when they try to take that Marshal's star from the likes of Cole Stockton. It will be like roping a grizzly. Once you got him, what are you going to do with him?"

CHAPTER THREE

"The Fugitives"

A few days later, I pulled Warrior up in front of the Denver Jail and dismounted. My feet were slightly numb from the cold, and I stomped some life back into them until I could wiggle my toes. I looped the reins around the hitching rack and Warrior looked at me like he hoped that I wouldn't be too long. I patted his head and assured him that we would seek out a nice warm stall just as soon as I found out what was going on.

I stepped into the jail. Three fancy dressed men sat around the desk drinking coffee. They turned as one to look me up and down.

"Who are you and what is your business with this office?"

"W-e-l-l, I understand that you are holding a good friend of mine here, and I would firstly like to speak with him. Secondly, I want to know just who the hell you dandies are and what your interest is in the Colorado Territory." That ruffled their feathers a mite.

They retorted with, "We'll ask the questions here. We're Special Agents sent by the U.S. Magistrate to take charge of the law here-a-bouts. Now, just who are you?"

"The name is *Cole Stockton*, and I AM the United States Marshal for Colorado. Bring the Judge out here."

"We'll take your badge, Stockton. You are dismissed. You can see MR. Wilkerson, but you will unbuckle your gunbelt and leave it here on this desk," the leader of the trio patted the desktop.

"Not likely," I replied.

Two of the men started to reach for their guns.

Now—I don't take well to fancy-dressed, Eastern strangers dragging iron on me, so I sharply interrupted them by suddenly producing my own Colt. I was considerably faster than they were.

"I wouldn't do that if I were you," I warned.

They hesitated with widened eyes.

With my revolver still trained on them, I was giving orders. "Now, let's get the Judge out here. I want to hear his story, and you three will listen—very carefully."

* *

Joshua Wilkerson grinned widely as the door to the cell block opened and all three Special Agents walked in, hands held high. Cole Stockton was right behind them.

"Well, fellers, I see that you have met Cole Stockton. I hope that you didn't try to draw your pistols. Most men that have tried it are dead and buried. You fellers are mighty lucky to be alive."

"Come on, Judge," Cole Stockton greeted his old friend. "This place doesn't suit you. We'll go someplace else and figure this thing out."

The Chief Special Agent turned to Joshua Wilkerson. "You can't escape from us. We will hunt you down and there will be even more charges against you."

"He's got a point there, Cole. The warrant seemed legal. I can't leave their custody or I'll look guilty."

"Well, Judge. Since you can't leave their custody, we'll just have to take them along with us. That way, you will always be with them. They will be unarmed, of course. Anyway, they can find out firsthand what the real West is like."

"I like that idea, Cole. We will have the pleasure of your company, gentlemen. I hope that you all can ride a horse, cause where we're going, there are no modern conveniences. Let's go, Cole."

"You are breaking jail," stated one of the men, as though that would change Cole Stockton's mind.

"No, Sir, I am not breaking jail. I am merely being escorted all over the Colorado countryside in the custody of my lawful keepers."

* *

Judge Wilkerson and I escorted the three Eastern lawmen down to the stables and commandeered mounts for each of them. Before we left, the Judge sent word to Marie through the livery stable hostler that he was okay: I was here. Once saddled up, I led out toward the wilds of the Lower Colorado.

I wanted to get these gents into the roughest country they had ever seen. They would get a definite taste of the truly Wild West.

Besides, this situation reeked of doings by that group known only by the term *The Association*.

The Association employed some pretty hard characters, and that there would be a shooting spree, I had no doubt. If this were the circumstances, I wanted to meet them on my own terms, out in the wilds so that no innocent bystander would get hurt.

Well, those three Easterners could ride—somewhat. About the fourth hour in the saddle, with close to freezing temperatures and knee-high snow on the ground, they were getting mighty wishful of a warm fire and something hot to drink.

Judge Wilkerson looked as if he was enjoying the ride. I kind of figured that he every so often daydreamed about riding out on the wild trails to hunt down *dirty rascals* himself.

The wilder the countryside got, the more he had that "gleam" in his eyes.

Finally, toward nightfall, I led our small party down into a sheltered ravine. It wound around and around until finally opening out into a small meadow.

I continued on until we were in a thick clump of pines, then halted.

I had the Agents dismount, unsaddle, and rub down the horses. They all had looks of disbelief on their faces.

"We're not staying here—are we?" asked the shortest, palest Easterner in shaky voice.

Judge Wilkerson grinned at me with a twinkle in his eyes. Whatever my answer, the Judge was going to enjoy it immensely.

"Yes. We are going to spend the night right here. It is too dangerous to ride this country at night—even for an experienced tracker. There are wild animals, and even hostile Indians on the prowl, not to mention a hundred other dangers such as falling off a cliff or into sudden crevices, or even a sudden freezing winter blizzard. Should any of this happen, we will endure it together. I want you to see and feel what the Judge and our men have had to put up with in searching out the scum of this country."

"Alright, walk around and gather up all the DRY wood you can find. Judge, grab up some snow in that coffee pot we brought with us. We'll have some coffee and a small meal of biscuits and jerky. We'll rest here for the night and continue on in the morning.

I didn't need to watch them. Where would they go? They sure as Hell didn't know where they were. Only I knew, and I liked it that way.

CHAPTER FOUR

"The Search Begins"

The leader of *The Association* stood with his back to the group to silently read the telegram to himself. His face turned from smiles to ashen-colored disbelief.

He turned to his associates.

"Gentlemen. We have trouble. Judge Wilkerson is missing from his jail cell since late yesterday afternoon and the three Special Agents from Washington are missing as well. With Wilkerson on the loose, they will no doubt attempt to track down the discrepancies that we forged and will be unraveling our plans. Our people will now have to find them and kill them all. We cannot afford to leave any witnesses to point in our direction."

Another member of the group, a man with bushy eyebrows and a pointed nose, spoke up.

"Let's issue a wanted poster on Wilkerson with, say, Five thousand dollars reward—make it read DEAD OR ALIVE. That should produce some information as to their whereabouts. We can have our own people serve as a posse and press the leads. They will leave no witnesses once we locate them."

"Good idea. We will have them distributed by tomorrow morning."

* *

Brant James led *The Association's* mercenary, illegal Posse of twenty hard-bitten men toward the wilds.

In all of the Colorado Territory there was one place that outlaw factions and other men on the run would instinctively head for—the Lower Colorado Wilds. There were hideouts galore.

The country was the roughest ever seen, and that made it quite attractive to wanted men. Trackers would have a difficult time following a trail, and in some cases a trailing posse could be seen or heard for miles in the still air.

James began his search for the elusive fugitives by making his own inquiries and was told by the Livery Hostler that Cole Stockton was leading his quarry. The reward posters were in Joshua Wilkerson's name, but his orders were to kill all found with him.

A certain gleam of fame entered into his mind's eye. He had the expertise as a bounty hunter to track this bunch down. If he could take Stockton, he would be famous. He would be the Top Gun of his profession.

That thought brought a crooked grin to his whiskered face as he lit up a *homemade*, drew deeply on it, and then exhaled a long stream of white-gray smoke.

His hazel eyes narrowed to mere slits as he pondered the direction that Stockton and the small group would go. He knew the trails out there, and he knew that it would come down to who could outsmart the other in this deadly game of cat and mouse.

* *

That first night out, we got a decent-sized fire going and those Eastern fellers did nothing but huddle around it. The Judge and I being Westerners moved back from the flames so that the brightness didn't lull us into a false sense of security.

A man who stares into the flames of his campfire can't see into the darkness should some danger suddenly present itself.

Furthermore, I was listening for sounds. Sounds that were supposed to be there; sounds like small animals scurrying through the night, owls, and yes, even the long, low, lonely howl of the timber wolf.

Their absence would signal immediate danger.

The night was long and cold and I could see that those fellers were having a hard time of it. They lay shivering in their city clothes and blankets. Well, in the morning I would lead them to one the homesteads I knew of. Jacob and Annie Osgood would no doubt enjoy the visit, and the Judge would be safe there himself for a while.

Daybreak came, and we saddled up. I led out toward the southwest and as we rode, I pointed out the beauty of nature that happened to show itself.

There was a mule ear deer family, a couple of eagles, an elk or two, a distant bear, and following at a distance, a couple of wolves.

It was, I reckon, about five in the evening when we entered the small clearing to find a lazy trail of wood smoke lifting from the chimney of that little cabin.

We rode up to the front door and you could smell coffee brewing. I hallowed the house and out stepped Jacob. A broad smile spread over his face and turning his head, he called back into the house for Annie, "Get some more plates down, Honey, we have visitors."

"Howdy, Marshal Stockton! We ain't seen you in a coon's age. Annie is just getting supper together and ya'll are welcome to join us."

Well, Annie loved it. She looked as if she had put on a few pounds in the months since I had last seen them and I hinted so.

"We are expecting our first child in about five months, Marshal, and Jacob is really excited about it."

Anyway, she fairly floated around that kitchen while she stirred up and added a few things to her venison stew pot and rolled out yet another sheet of her wonderful biscuits. It seems that Annie also had a freshly baked false apple pie cooling on the window sill.

It was called *False Apple Pie* because when apples were scarce, frontier cooks would use potatoes sliced very thin and seasoned like a real apple pie. Done right, a man could not tell the difference. Annie was one of those cooks that just naturally put together some mighty tasty meals. Of course, there was always a fresh pot of good hot black coffee.

Once supper was on the table, the Easterners dug right on in and they ate like they hadn't had a good meal since they left Washington, D.C.

The Osgoods were good folks and had been through some rough times to keep this small homestead.

They had fought off night raiders together, and when the law finally came into this territory, they did all they could to help.

Mostly, for my part, they fixed me up with a hot meal and a good night's sleep when I needed it.

Jacob and Annie spoke of their appreciation of frontier law and order to the Eastern lawmen. They told of the way it used to be and of the way it was presently, with Judge Wilkerson's lawmen and his court weeding out the spoilers.

Jacob spoke up. "It takes a good man with a gun and the sense to use it to read the law into some, and the Judge's Marshals and Deputies are the kind of men that are willing and able to do just that. If it were not for the likes of Marshal Stockton, why, we might be dead and buried some time ago."

I began to see a slight change in the Easterners mannerisms, like they were just beginning to understand something.

We finished our meal and I laid out the situation to Jacob and Annie. They eagerly invited the Judge and his *keepers* to stay with them while I did some investigating on my own.

* *

Brant James split his "Posse" of twenty riders into four groups. Each group would take a quadrant of the wilds and ride back and forth looking for sign.

Should any tracks of a small party the size of Judge Wilkerson's party be found, they would follow the tracks until recognition, then, they would send riders to get the other groups.

Brant James wanted to be in on the kill. He wanted Stockton for himself and as much told the others.

James recollected then that Stockton seemed to make his headquarters in a small town along the passes between the Lower Colorado and the upper New Mexico border. James decided to take his group of five and stop in there. He might just pick up some information as to the whereabouts of the fugitives.

They could also pick up some supplies and additional ammunition. They might need it.

* *

With the Judge and those Easterners settled down in their temporary safe place, I swung into the saddle and headed south toward Laura's ranch. I also wanted to stop in and see J.C. and appraise him of the situation. J.C. might've picked up some valuable information for me as well.

Warrior and I were about five hours from the cabin when I found the trail of a large group of shod horses. They were traveling kind of slow and spread out some like they were hunting for something.

"A posse of some sort," I thought, "Probably looking for the Judge and his company."

I decided to follow the trail a bit and after a few miles or so, the group split into four smaller groups. None of them were headed directly in the Judge's direction, so I figured we still had some time.

I thought hard about what I would do if I were leading that posse.

I would split the group and crisscross the land looking for sign of a party about our size. I also reckoned that no group of five was going to try and take the Judge's party by themselves. No, they would send for the other groups to be in force when they struck.

I noticed that one group led off toward the lower passes and J.C. Kincaid's town. I decided to follow this bunch.

* *

Judge Wilkerson and his small party sat around the warm fire in the Osgood's cabin and played cards. The Judge smiled as he raked in another pot. They were playing for matches, but he was pleased that his skill at poker hadn't diminished any in the past few years since his arrival in the Colorado Territory.

Annie Osgood kept them supplied with hot coffee and baked goods. She even sat in on a couple of hands of poker.

Annie had worked in a saloon before she met Jacob and married him. She was having the time of her life. They hadn't had too many visitors out here in the wilds. The story of these unusual visitors would make for lots of good town conversation and surprising letters to her family.

Annie loved the wilds. It was peaceful most of the time, and she got to see nature at first hand. There were deer families that passed close to the cabin now and then. There was a small creek that ran about fifty yards in back, and during the warm months, she and Jacob would sit lazily on the banks and fish together—rifle and shotgun close at hand.

Once, she even saw a Southern Cheyenne warrior sitting his pony in the distance. How fierce he looked!

The warrior didn't venture any closer, but seemed to be studying their home and how they had taken care of it.

Jacob had planted a small vegetable garden. He hunted for meat and they used everything that they could. They tried to give back to the land and not spoil it.

Annie told Jacob about the warrior that she had seen, and he cautioned her to be ever watchful, but nothing ever happened. It was like the Indians deliberately left them alone because they appeared to love the land as much as the savages themselves.

CHAPTER FIVE

"Posse's on the Move"

Laura Lynne Sumner saddled up Mickey and rode toward Miller's Station. She carried a small shopping list, and she would check at the post office for any mail.

Cole Stockton had been gone for several days now, and there was no word. Perhaps, J.C. Kincaid had word from Cole. She would stop in at the jail and see.

An hour later found Laura in front of the jail. She entered and smiled brightly at J.C. who sat frowning over *WANTED POSTERS* on his desk.

"Good morning, J.C. A great morning, isn't it?"

"Morning, Laura. I sure wish that it were. Look here. I just received these on this morning's stage. *Wanted* posters on Joshua Wilkerson. They don't even call him a Judge anymore, just a sorely wanted man. They even offer five thousand dollars for him—DEAD OR ALIVE, or a thousand dollars for information leading to his capture. It says that he broke jail up at the Denver Jail and kidnapped the three Eastern special lawmen that were sent to take him."

Laura added her thoughts, "J.C., if Judge Wilkerson is missing, then, Cole is with him and they probably have those Easterners with them. It sounds like Cole is trying to hide those men, or at least keep them from something or someone until he can straighten this mess out. It is obviously some sort of mistake, and Cole will set it straight. By the way, have you heard from Cole since he left five days ago?"

"No, Laura, I have no words on Cole, but I did hear that two of the Judge's Marshals were relieved of their authority and dismissed. I wired Toby Bodine up in Creede, and advised him to keep a sharp eye on things up there. Cole asked me to keep my eyes and ears open for peculiar things around here. Up to now, I haven't detected anything out of the ordinary."

It was at that very moment that a small group of six hard-looking riders trotted up to the jail and the leader dismounted.

Brant James entered the jail. He slowly and appreciatively looked over Laura Sumner, then turned his attention to J.C. Kincaid.

Laura felt the man's eyes on her, and she formed an instant dislike for him.

"Sheriff, I am Brant James. I have been appointed to lead a posse in search of the former Judge Wilkerson and three Eastern special agents which Wilkerson and Cole Stockton have kidnapped. I understand that Stockton makes this town his headquarters. Have you seen or heard from him in the past few days? If you have, it would be wise to cooperate. We will track them down and see justice done."

J.C. Kincaid knew what that meant.

He had heard of James, and the word was that he was a vicious killer. His reputation as a bounty hunter was such that none of his *bounty* ever reached court alive.

Laura was suddenly fearful for Cole, the Judge, and those other men, but she held her composure and kept silent.

"No, Mr. James, I haven't heard from Marshal Stockton in the past five days."

"By the way, it isn't MARSHAL STOCKTON anymore. All of Wilkerson's Marshals and Deputies have been dismissed. We are the Territorial law now, and I want those men. Do you understand?"

"Yeah, James, I understand. Right now you are in MY TOWN. I am the ELECTED law here, and in this town, your authority doesn't mean a hill of beans to me. You want Stockton, you go and find him, and I hope you find him because Cole Stockton will set you and your kind straight on the law around this Territory."

"You calling me out, Sheriff? I don't think that you are good enough to take me, but if you want to try, step out that door."

J.C. glared at James, and started to rise.

20

THE STOCKTON SAGA 5

Laura immediately saw the danger and spoke up. "Not now, J.C."

Kincaid stopped after rising and stared straight into Brant James' eyes.

"Some other time, James. I have things to do right now. You have made your point, and we understand each other."

"Just be sure you get word to me if you hear ANYTHING about Stockton."

Brant James turned and with a crooked grin towards Laura Sumner walked out the door, slamming it behind him.

J.C. Kincaid looked at Laura.

"Thanks, Laura. I guess I sort of lost my head. James is quite known for his gunplay and he may be right. I don't know if I can take him or not. Anyway, I think that this is some of that *peculiar* information that Cole was looking for. I have heard that James has acquaintances with rather dark and mysterious connections. I wonder if he is working for *The Association*. Let me send some telegrams. I have some friends who may have information valuable to this situation. You watch yourself, Laura. This thing is bigger than we think."

"J.C., I'm going to get some of my boys and ride out to where I think Cole was headed. I may just run into him and then we'll see about this Mr. Brant James."

* *

Laura stepped out the door of the jail and suddenly saw Cole Stockton riding into town. She looked quickly in the other direction and the six men of the posse were just reining in at Booker's General Store to get their supplies.

She frantically hailed Cole Stockton to her.

"Cole! You can't be here right now. Those six men in front of Booker's Store are part of a murder posse out looking for you and the Judge. They are led by a man named Brant James, and he has his eye out for you. He said that you are no longer the U.S. Marshal, and that all the Judge's Marshals were dismissed."

"They were, Laura. But, I am NOT one of the Judge's Marshals.

I AM the UNITED STATES MARSHAL for the Lower Colorado. Judge Wilkerson didn't appoint me. Get J.C. and let's not keep that bunch waiting. I want to see to them as well." Laura turned back to the jail to get Sheriff Kincaid.

* *

Brant James dismounted and stepped up with his men on the boardwalk in front of Booker's Store. He stretched his stiff muscles and slowly looked around. His face suddenly flushed, his jaw dropped open slightly and his eyes went wide with disbelief. It was like seeing a ghost!

Cole Stockton was briskly walking straight toward them, followed by J.C. Kincaid about ten steps behind. About five steps behind Sheriff Kincaid was that woman.

Kincaid carried a double-barreled Express shotgun, and the woman held a Winchester in her hands.

Brant James hadn't noticed it before, but the woman was also wearing a gun, slung like she knew how to use it.

"James! Brant James!" called out Cole Stockton. "I understand that you are looking for me! Well, here I am! You and your friends are under arrest for conspiracy to commit the murder of a Federal Judge and Federal Officers. You can drop your guns or drag iron and it don't make much difference to me."

Brant James now thought quickly. Could he take Stockton?

He had bragged to his men as to just how fast he was and that he was going to be the man who would take Stockton.

He looked nervously at his five men.

If all six of them drew, they could take the man, or could they? Stockton had a reputation for standing against all odds.

Suddenly two of his men reached down and unbuckled their gunbelts letting them drop to the ground. They moved away from the others.

The remaining three men decided to try it and their hands flashed for their revolvers.

Brant James unconsciously found his own hand reaching for his gun butt.

His hand grasped the smooth grips, his finger slipping into the trigger guard, his thumb cocking the revolver as it rose. It was sliding out of the holster, rising to line on Stockton.

The other three armed men in the posse filled their hands with pistol grips and their revolvers were also rising out of their holsters. Their faces were grim with the ugly task at hand.

They were going to finally kill U.S. Marshal Cole Stockton, or die trying.

J.C. Kincaid saw the rapid movements and leveled the shotgun directly at the three men. His thumb cocked both of the hammers back in one fluid motion and his finger began the smooth squeezing of the dual triggers.

Laura Sumner quickly levered a .30 caliber bullet into the chamber of her Winchester and was bringing it to bear on the center man of the three.

All eyes were on Cole Stockton as his right hand blurred to his holster.

The walnut-gripped Colt rose fluidly up and out, smoothly rising to level directly at Brant James. Stockton's left hand moved almost as fast to form a palming action over the hammer of the leveling revolver. Stockton was going to *fan the Colt*.

Brant James stared incredulously as the bore of Stockton's Colt spit flame and hot lead—first at him, then to the next man, and the next, and the next, until each of the four men staggered backwards with the impact of deadly lead in rapid succession.

The shotgun boomed almost at the same instant and deadly 20gauge shot sprayed the three men standing to the left of James. The center man also jerked up on his toes and slammed back to lie grotesquely still as the .30 caliber slug took him deep in the chest.

A moment later, all was still. A dark cloud of gunsmoke hovered over the scene.

Brant James lay with fire in his chest. He was the only one of the four still alive. Neither he nor any of his men had fired a shot. They lay where they fell, cocked revolvers still in their hands.

U.S. Marshal Cole Stockton slowly walked up to Brant James. His revolver was cocked for the fifth time. He looked down at James, then bent down and took the unfired revolver from him.

"You'll live to stand trial James, I wanted you alive. Want to stand alone, or will you talk? I want names, circumstances, and whereabouts. The doctor will be here shortly."

James groaned with pain, but managed to speak. "I only know one of the group called *The Association*. The name is Frank Stark. At the last telegraph message, he was in Omaha at the Cattleman's Hotel. There is some sort of big meeting going on and it has to do with getting rid of the Judge. That's all I know."

"I'll see what I can do for you, James," Stockton softened. "Here comes the Doc now. You will be guarded well while you are mending and then go to J.C. Kincaid's jail."

CHAPTER SIX

"Justice for the Judge"

I turned to J.C. Kincaid and asked him to take over seeing to Brant James and the others.

"Laura, I need some help. I need you to bring every wrangler you can spare up to the Osgood homestead just as fast as you can. I am sending a telegram to Clay; then I am riding hell bent to the Osgood's homestead. There are about fifteen other hard men searching the wilds for the Judge, and they will be getting closer by now. I hope to beat them there."

"Of course, Cole, I can bring eight—with rifles. We'll be only an hour or so behind you. "Cole," she paused until their eyes met, "you be careful."

* *

I sent a telegram to my brother, Clay, advising him of Frank Stark and his connection to *The Association*. Clay was the U.S. Marshal in Bismarck, but he had associates in Omaha and could work that situation.

I knew Frank and suddenly the plot came together. Frank Stark was a highly aggressive cattle baron in the central New Mexico Territory. Rumor had it that he was running out of land with water to hold his massive herds on, and it made a lot of sense that he would be looking for more land—good land.

The Lower Colorado wilds had everything. There were good grass, water, and even canyons to pen up stock in—natural corrals.

Money and power sometimes make people think that they are above the law. Frank Stark would stop at nothing to expand his domain.

That included running innocent folks off their hard worked land, and forcing them to sell at rock bottom prices.

I swung into the saddle and Warrior seemed to sense the urgency of the ride. He jumped straight into an easy gallop and we were off to the wilds.

* *

Judge Wilkerson, Annie Osgood, and the three Eastern Special Agents were having a good time visiting. They were enjoying the coffee and Annie's cookies when Jacob suddenly burst into the cabin.

"Everybody get ready. There is a large passel of riders working their way up slope toward us. They will be at this clearing within thirty minutes. We must be ready for anything. Judge, I think that this is a posse out to do you in. They all look like rough, hard men—not the kind that you would want in a normal law-abiding posse." And, then Jacob added, "These men look a lot like the raiders that we knew so well."

Judge Wilkerson looked seriously at the three Eastern men.

"You men are about to see firsthand just what lawlessness is. There is only one way to handle it out here, and that is with hard, willing men and hot lead. Do you want to help?"

Without hesitation, the three chose to defend the Osgood's home. Judge Wilkerson handed them their pistols back, saying,"Them pea shooters aren't much good at long range. Wait until they get in close. Jacob, let me have one of your rifles. I used to be quite handy at dropping game. Show us where you want us."

Firstly, the Eastern lawmen were astounded when Annie reached up and took down HER rifle, a .30 caliber Winchester saddle gun. She saw their looks and smiled, saying, "Haven't you ever seen a woman defend her own home? I can shoot, and shoot good."

Secondly, Jacob handed the Judge a .44 Caliber Henry Repeater and a belt of ammunition. Jacob himself took a .56 caliber Sharps buffalo gun and a belt of cartridges. He also wore his Colt Navy .44 strapped around his waist. He put his two cents worth in as well, "Yes, Sir, Annie is quite a marksman. She can outshoot me."

Within minutes, fifteen or so ugly, mean-looking riders boiled into the clearing. They rode up to the door of the cabin and yelled out. "You in the cabin, come out with your hands up. We won't ask again."

Annie looked over at Jacob. He grinned at her and shouted though the wooden shutters, "Go to Hell!"

Fifteen hard-bitten men reached for their weapons. Flame, hot lead, and yells split the din. Gunsmoke drifted in the air.

All six of the occupants fired immediately and five men were driven off their horses to lie in various manner of either death or wounds on the cold hard ground.

The remaining ten riders pulled back to the outer circle of the clearing and began a hot masking rifle fire at the small cabin.

Bullets whizzed through the shutters and smacked into walls. The outer walls of the cabin took lead as well, and splinters flew everywhere.

The Eastern lawmen were wide—eyed in the beginning at this kind of thing happening, but all three were determined. They returned fire just like Annie, Jacob, and Judge Wilkerson.

The Judge was having a good ole day. He yelled his enthusiasm each time he fired.

The cabin filled with the acrid smell of gunsmoke amid the sharp cracks of Annie's Winchester, the thundering crack of the Judge's Henry, and the heavy boom of the Sharps. The three Eastern pistols were sort of *popping* in between, creating a symphony of deadly magnitude.

Four hours went by and ammunition inside the small cabin was dwindling dreadfully low.

Annie thought she saw movement coming from the right side. She squinted down the barrel of her Winchester and was about to squeeze off when she recognized the horse and rider.

"Jacob! Quick! Get ready to open the door. Here comes Marshal Stockton at a gallop."

Jacob Osgood unbarred the heavy wooden door. He peeked through a crack and at just the right moment, he threw it open and fired a loud boom into the posse's middle.

Cole Stockton slid Warrior to a quick halt, jumped out of the saddle, and dashed into the cabin with saddlebags and Winchester in hand.

Warrior bolted into a quick run and within moments was out of sight.

Jacob threw the door shut and barred it. He turned to Cole Stockton with a grin on his face.

"Just like old times, huh, Marshal?"

"You got me there, Jacob. How are we doing?"

Judge Wilkerson spoke up, "I ain't had so much fun in years, Cole, but we are getting mighty short on cartridges. Did you bring any?"

"Well, I got about fifty rounds of Winchester .44, fifty rounds of Winchester .30, and a lot of .45. I think we can hold them for an hour or so. Laura Sumner and her wranglers will be here shortly and then, we'll take this shindig to them and they aren't going to like it. Annie, got any coffee ready, I could sure use a cup."

Annie laughed, knowing Cole and his love of coffee.

"Always the coffee, Cole! You must live on the stuff. Pots on the stove, help yourself."

* *

It was within the hour that the surrounding posse decided to burn the cabin, if they could get some torches close enough.

They found Jacob's old wagon, parked next to his stables. They piled it with brush and set it on fire.

They were pushing it toward the least protected side of the cabin when numerous sharp cracks split the air.

Eight or nine riders were lined along the edge of the clearing and firing directly into the posse.

The door of the cabin literally flew open and Cole Stockton, Judge Wilkerson, Jacob Osgood, and all three of the Eastern lawmen dashed out into the open. They all had pre-planned positions and they spread out firing as fast as they could into the remnants of the posse.

Within ten minutes the posse members were either dead, wounded, or throwing their arms into the air.

Laura Sumner and her wranglers rode behind the surviving posse members and forced them into the cabin yard. They found themselves subsequently arrested by Cole Stockton and the Federal Agents.

The Agents and Jacob tied up the living members, and laid out the dead.

Special Agent Grant Newsome faced Joshua Wilkerson. He held out his hand.

"JUDGE Wilkerson, consider yourself reinstated. The documents will follow as soon as I report back to Washington, but I want you to know that we learned something here. The West needs men like yours to wear the star. I wouldn't have believed it if I hadn't seen it with my own eyes and fought alongside you and these good folks. There have been some grave misunderstandings and we will set them right. There will also be an investigation in Washington. There was political pressure from somewhere, and we will find those responsible. There will be justice."

Jacob and Annie Osgood stood together side by side, arms around each other. They had survived yet another deadly adventure in the wilds.

Cole Stockton put his arm around Laura, looked deeply into her crystal blue eyes and softly said, "Well, Laura, this time YOU arrived in the nick of time."

Laura smiled back at him, thought for only a moment and replied,

"I suppose that's the way it's always going to be. Each of us saving the other—in the nick of time. I love you, Cole Stockton."

The kiss was warm and those standing nearby could almost feel the smoldering passion of their love for each other, so they turned away or pulled their hats over their eyes out of respect.

* *

Five well-dressed men sat grimly facing each other in the Omaha Hotel office room and spoke in low tones when a knock came at the door.

One of the men got up to answer it.

The door suddenly burst open to admit four men wearing Silver Stars on their coats. They held drawn revolvers.

The tall, lanky leader turned to the five men. He announced, "Gentlemen, I am Clay Stockton, United States Marshal, and these men are MY Deputies. I have a FEDERAL WARRANT for the arrest of Frank Stark, Nathan Evans, Charles Newberry, Olin Forrest, and Marcus Kanaday, otherwise known as The *Association*."

Clay Stockton waited a moment before continuing, "The charges are: falsifying legal documents, conspiracy to defame and murder a Federal Judge and Federal Officers, bribing officials of the United States government, and soliciting persons to commit murder. The rest is purely personal."

Clay held a wry grin on his face as he announced, "You can come peaceably, or you can drag iron, and we don't care which."

CHAPTER SEVEN

"Ambush"

Toward the end of spring it seemed that the snows of winter had dissipated. Streams were filled to their banks with fresh running cold waters, and teeming with fish. The land was rejuvenating itself in preparation for the annual planting event.

Bismarck, North Dakota established in 1872, was known as an outlaw town with no law and no limits. Years later, law came to the rail town.

On this particular night, the streets of Bismarck were dim and empty. Even the rowdiest of the saloons had only a few customers at this hour. Only the staunchest drinker and card player remained at the bar and at the gambling tables.

Two cigarettes glowed softly in the darkness of the alley where two hard men waited in grim silence for their victim. One spoke softly to the other, "Suppose he don't come down this side of the street tonight. What do we do then?"

"He always comes down this side of the street, and always around the same time—between two and three in the morning. Our orders are to take him. That's why those guys paid us the two hundred dollars. Ha, they said that no one could take this man. We'll show them."

Momentarily, they heard the soft jingling of spurs. Someone was coming up the boardwalk on their side of the street. They readied themselves. Could this be the man?

The tall, lanky figure walked steadily as he checked doors to businesses and peered into saloons. There seemed to be no trouble

31

afoot this evening. Everything was quiet. That gave him an uneasy feeling, but he walked with determined steps to the next block.

He stepped off the boardwalk at the alley entrance, and even as he heard the click of metal against metal, he was drawing his Colt. The two men levered their Winchesters and fired almost as one at the shadowed figure with the Silver Star of the U.S. Marshal on his vest.

They watched their man jerk with the impact of two .44-40 rounds as the heavy lead thunked into him. The Marshal slammed to the ground and they fired a second time, watching his body jerk with the impact of two more rifle bullets. The Marshal had drawn his weapon but not fired. The Colt lay cocked in his limp hand.

The two men moved cautiously forward. They were to make sure that this man <u>Clay Stockton</u> was DEAD. They stepped closer to him.

Suddenly, Stockton's eyes glared open with life and his Colt Revolver cracked twice. The two ambushers jerked backward with the impact of .44 caliber lead at point blank range, then fell straight down in the muddy street to lay almost beside the man they were sent to kill.

U.S. Marshal Clay Stockton lay immobilized with pain as he tried to cock his Colt once again. He had taken four rifle bullets at fairly close range. He was hit in his right thigh, his right side, a long furrow along his stomach and one that whined through his rib cage to break opposite ribs as the bullet exited the other side.

Two shabbily dressed strangers lay within four feet of him, both shot through the heart. Even at this late hour, people were filling the street. Deputy U.S. Marshal Sandy Merrick was suddenly beside him, "Clay! Dammit, Clay, speak to me! You somebitch, don't you die on me. You got two men, Clay, is that all? Was there more? Tell me dammit, don't you close your eyes, talk to me!"

Merrick yelled out as loud as he could, "<u>SOMEONE GET THE DOCTOR OUT HERE</u>, the Marshal is hit bad." Then to his friend, "Aw Clay, come on, talk to me, come on, say something."

Deputy Merrick held Clay Stockton's head in his arms and listened closely as he hoarsely, almost whispered, "Sandy, get Cole here as fast as you can. He is in Helena, Montana right now and can be here within three days if he hurries. God, it hurts. Get me off this street."

Deputy Merrick assured Clay that he would summon Cole immediately and then began again, "Clay, stay with us. Here comes Doc now. You rest easy, I'll wire Cole for you. DON'T YOU DIE ON ME, I ain't got my pay for this month yet."

Clay Stockton for all his hurt grinned against the pain, "I couldn't have said it better myself." And then he passed out.

Deputy U.S. Marshal Sandy Merrick watched the doctor and several men carry his boss to the doctor's makeshift hospital. The Bismarck Town Marshal and the local Sheriff stepped up to him. Both men were somber looking.

"What did he say to you before he passed out?" asked Town Marshal Tom Kolbert.

Sheriff John Ranger kept silent and seemed a bit nervous.

"He told me to watch you two somebitches, cause you are as crooked as the games in the saloons. We both know that you rake percentages from the cheating that you allow, and one day we will prove it. We will rip the badges right off your shirts and put you where you belong, that is, if you don't draw against us. You always got that chance, and by God right now I wish that either one or both of you would just <u>tickle</u> iron."

"Is that a threat, Merrick? We'll arrest you for making threats like that."

"It's more of a promise, Tom. Within three days you two are going to have more misery than you can ever imagine. I personally think that you figured to have those two dead men kill Marshal Stockton, and then maybe try and kill me. Well, here I am, that is, iffen you two together think that I am any easier than Clay. There is nothing I'd like better than to take down two appointed henchmen in one swipe. Who shall I bill for your burial?"

"You are treading on thin ice, Merrick. Stockton was brash and stepped heavy on some big toes. You, however, are small fish. There is more at stake here than what you think. By the way, I can take you any time you want. What do you think of that?"

"I think you're overloading your mouth, Tom. Want to try now?" Sandy challenged.

"You aren't worth the lead, or the bother. Stockton will die from his wounds, and then, you'd best get yourself out of this town. We run things here, and don't you forget it."

"No, Tom. You listen. Like I said, in about three days, whether I'm still alive or not, you and your kind will have more trouble than you can handle."

Sandy waited a moment before continuing, "There's a man going to be riding here that don't take lightly to people shooting down his kinfolk, especially his brother. Were I you, I'd just pack my kit and light a shuck out of this territory, or even out of the country, maybe Canada. Just look back over your shoulder either way because he might just be right behind you. You have never seen the likes of this man. Clay Stockton would give a man a chance to surrender. This man will shoot you where he finds you, and leave your sorry carcasses for the scavengers. Why, I've heard tell that he took on seven men in the Waco, Texas Short Horn Saloon when he was younger. He took lead, but he killed all seven of them."

"That would be Cole Stockton, if I recall rightly," said Sheriff John Ranger, with a somewhat weak and shaky voice.

"I'd say that you are about right," answered Deputy U.S. Marshal Merrick as he looked up from examining the two dead men. He held two hundred dollars in his hand.

"So, this is what a U.S. Marshal's life is worth? Tell your gambling friends that I want them ALL to hang for the attempted murder of a Federal Marshal. They have three days to turn themselves in or pay the consequences," demanded Merrick.

"Merrick, you won't live three days."

"Well, Tom, let's get it on. I know that you are just itching. Let's see if you can take a <u>small fish</u> Deputy, face to face instead of from ambush."

The Town Marshal intentionally kept his hands away from his guns. He knew Sandy Merrick from reputation, and Sandy, although not as fast as Clay Stockton, was fairly lethal. Tom Kolbert would take no chances. There were others that he could find to take the chance.

* *

Laura Sumner, Johanna Stockton, and U.S. Marshal Cole Stockton were enjoying a breakfast of crisp bacon, fried eggs, fried potatoes, and a stack of *buckwheat pancakes* in the Helena Hotel restaurant when the telegraph runner dashed up to them. In an almost out of breath chant, he related the words that set Cole Stockton's heart blazing with vengeance.

"Marshal Stockton! Your brother Clay was shot from ambush. He is near death and wants you to ride to Bismarck immediately. Deputy U.S. Marshal Merrick requests that you hurry with all speed and dispatch."

Without hesitation, Stockton directed the telegraph runner "Wire Deputy Merrick back that I will be there in two days."

"I'm going with you!" resounded Johanna.

"Cole, I'm going, too," stated Laura immediately. "Nothing you can say can keep either Johanna or me from riding with you. When do we leave?"

"We leave within the hour. Mother, keep faith. Clay is alive, I feel it in my bones. Either way, there will be *Justice*. If the law doesn't do it, I WILL."

Two hours later found the small party of three on the trail from Helena, Montana to Bismarck, North Dakota. They trailed a pack horse as they did from Southern Colorado to the Montana Territory. They rode, each with personal thoughts of their SON, BROTHER, and FRIEND.

* *

Cole thought back as they rode towards the town of Bismarck. "I remembered the times that Clay and I hunted together. Clay was always the meat provider. That is, that he was always better with a rifle than me. Nine times out of ten, it was his bullet that bagged the elk, deer, or antelope.

"I was infinitely better with the shorter range. I dearly loved handguns. Don't get me wrong, I was a fairly good shot at long range with the rifle—Pa saw to that, but my calling was the Colt Revolver. I guess that Pa saw it in me from the very first. He had me practice with his old Colt Patterson until I could hit each and every target first and every time.

"Clay was different. He dearly loved the long guns. His love was hunting—hunting for meat, and the thrill of the hunt. He was in his mid-twenties when he came to me and asked if I would teach him some revolver skills. Little did I know that he would become somewhat second to none when it came to slinging lead with a Colt. He sort of patterned himself after me, always carrying two Colts, one in his holster, and one in his belt behind his back, just in case."

Yah, I thought a lot about Clay. The more I thought about it, the madder I got. This was no known gunfight. These people had shot him from ambush. These men were cowards, or were so prominent that they wanted no mention of their names to such deeds. They might have hired it done. My thoughts turned to sheer hatred.

I admire a man that would face my brother and drag iron, no matter the consequences. Of course, family pride dictated that I would have to face such a man should my brother die, but that was something else to be reckoned with. Right now, it seemed that I was dealing with frightened men who wanted a good lawman out of the way. Why? I would find out and bring them to justice or death, their choice.

* *

Johanna was deep in thought as she rode silently along the trail beside Laura. "I was scared for my son, Clay. I knew not what his actual condition was, but I felt that it was very serious. I felt his pain deep in my breast, and although Cole tried his best to comfort me with words of reassurance, I knew that Clay's life was in danger. I sort of felt that he knew it, too. That's why he pushed us to ride faster and keep up with him. It wasn't until Laura and I both ganged up on him, that he did relent and let us stop for a small supper of coffee, beef jerky, and cold biscuits. I could see vengeance burning in his eyes. I had seen my oldest son with cold eyes before, during raids on our small ranch in West Texas when he defended us single- handedly against twelve raiding Comanche warriors.

"Back then, Cole wouldn't let up. He fired that old Colt Revolver until the barrel grew hot, then, he grabbed up that old flintlock pistol of my father's, loaded it, and stood ready to defend.

The Rangers came then, and saved us all. Cole was only twelve or so at the time, but I saw the determination in his eyes. I also saw something else. Cole was fast. He was faster than his father when it came to aiming, shooting, and reloading."

A thought crossed my mind then. "My son is a natural born killer—a gunman." My mind conjured up all sorts of vicious thoughts then. I tried to teach him right from wrong, and I think that my words instilled a unique sense of JUSTICE in him. I know that he is a hard man when it comes to the gun, but sometimes I have seen compassion from him. Like the time when he walked up to a young wounded Apache that he had shot during a raid. Cole walked calmly up to him, pointed the revolver straight at the warrior's face, then eased the hammer down. He held out his hand to the offending attacker and nursed him back to health.

The warrior never forgot that. Cole could have killed him right then and there. But, the Apache in return taught Cole the ways of the Apache, the life of the Apache, and the fears of the Apache.

Although my youngest son Clay was lying shot and hurt, my greatest concern at the moment was for my oldest son, Cole. I knew how he felt about his brother and the thoughts that plagued my mind were, "Devil take the slowest," rather than the law see justice. I worried over this dilemma as we rode."

* *

Laura Sumner also let her mind wander into the depth of her heart. "I felt sorrow for my best friend as we rode the trails toward North Dakota. Cole was strong, but there was something in his being that I hadn't seen since that day that I got shot over the sheep herding incident two years ago.

"He had that look in his eyes. It was as if he didn't care about the law, he just wanted to kill those responsible. I was glad that I had come along—somehow, I thought, I may be able to stop him from doing something that he would regret. Cole was meant to uphold the law, not use it to his own advantage as some did."

"Cole Stockton was good with the gun, sometimes too good, but I always saw justice in what he did. This time it was different. There was a hunger for vengeance in his eyes that told me that he might just circumvent the law and that bothered me."

Chapter Eight

"New Law in Town"

Deputy U.S. Marshal Sandy Merrick walked quietly down the hall of the upstairs hospital facility of the Bismarck Hotel. He stopped outside the closed door, took a deep breath and exhaled. A moment later, he turned the doorknob and stepped inside.

Clay Stockton lay seemingly asleep in the bed next to the single window. He was bandaged around his right thigh and his upper torso. He appeared pale and weak.

Sandy grabbed up a chair and sat down next to the seriously wounded U.S. Marshal. He watched him silently for several minutes then, softly spoke.

"Well, Clay, at least you are still alive. We buried them two scavengers this morning. Man, that was some shooting—on the ground, wounded and drilled them both right through the heart. Cole is on his way and I suspect that he will be here sometime tomorrow."

He hesitated for a few moments before continuing with soft voice, "I maybe shouldn't have, but I confronted Tom Kolbert and John Ranger about the gambling skims. They got pretty tiffed off and wanting to put scare into me. They mentioned that you stepped on some mighty big toes. They also threatened that I wouldn't live through the next three days. W-e-l-l, we'll see about that. First sign of trouble, I'm going straight to Tom and fill his ugly carcass with lead.

I know that I ain't been with you but three months now, Clay, but I shore wish that you had confided in me with this other stuff. It might help me piece together just why they, and I know it was them, had you drygulched."

Sandy grinned widely as he imparted his next bit of banter to the silent figure of his boss, "Hah! You should have seen their faces when I dropped the notion that I should take both of them out right then. They shore didn't like it, me facing them off and such. I'll have to watch myself quite close now, as I suspect that they are hatching a *surprise* for me. No matter. I'll do like you and take a few with me."

Sandy waited a few minutes before continuing, "Dammit, Clay, I'll say it again—DON'T you die on me, you somebitch. You are the best friend I got. Matter of fact, when you get out of this here hospital, I will buy you the biggest steak we can find, that is, if you will get me my pay for last month."

Sandy chuckled to himself then, reached up and squeezed Clay Stockton's hand. He was surprised when the hand squeezed back—firmly.

He looked Clay Stockton directly in the face and grinned when groggy brown eyes flicked open. A determined light shined within and Sandy knew that Stockton was going to come through all of this. He was too damn stubborn to die.

"You faker! I ought to make you get your sorry butt out of that bed and make the rounds tonight. You just laid there and let me make a fool out've myself—imagine telling YOU that you are my best friend. Ah, now I know what got you awake—that steak dinner I mentioned. You always like your steak. Well, I'll make you a better deal. When we get these guys, I'll take you to meet this old Injun I know. We'll have a few snorts, and hunt some deer or elk. You know, relax for a few days, do some hunting, drinking, and tell some good ole whoppers. You get well now, I got to go and get them boys a bit more worried."

Clay swallowed hard and grabbed Sandy's hand. He uttered as best as possible the information that sealed his ambush.

"Sandy. The—gambling—is just—is just—a front. The big winners are their own men. They pay them off in stolen gold from Canadian mines. Their men take the gold and ride to different towns to turn it into cold cash."

Clay swallowed hard and after a few moments of deep breathing and a few sips of water, continued, "There is a ring of operators from

Canada to the States. The Mounties are trying to stop this ring—and—and, we are to be a part of it. The suspected main ringleader here is Glen Turnbull, owner of the Rocking Cross Ranch. He has the mules and horses to transport the gold. His second in command is Nate Osborne, owner of the Eureka Saloon. Nate does the actual dispersing of the gold. We have to prove it in order to take them."

Sandy took a minute before replying, "Well, Boss, it's about time you told me about that trip you took to Canada a few weeks ago. I sure wish that you had told me sooner, Clay. We would have had these guys almost sewed up by now. Why, with my outbursts of outrageous challenges, they'd have come right at us—with both barrels. You and I could have shot hell out of them right in the street and taken the survivors to jail. Tom Kolbert and John Ranger right along with them."

He continued, "I sure don't like them boys none, and mark my words, one of these days, I will put lead into Tom Kolbert and bury that somebitch. John Ranger will most probably run. I think that he will crack first. He seemed mighty nervous that you were still alive that night, and even more so that you sent them two bushwackers to hell. Tom, now, he was cocky."

Sandy swallowed before he commented further, "Kolbert thinks he is the *top rooster* on the wall. Well, like I said, Clay, when the time comes—I want Tom. You rest now and get well. Cole will be here soon and then, I suspect that all hell will break loose."

* *

It was roughly two days later when a trail-weary threesome rode into Bismarck, North Dakota. They rode directly to the main hotel and tied up.

Cole Stockton turned to the two women and said, "Register for rooms. I am going to the jail and talk to Deputy Marshal Merrick. I'll be back directly and then we'll go and see Clay. Plan on a good dinner tonight; it will probably be the last for a while."

He turned abruptly and strode, spurs jingling, toward the jailhouse.

Johanna turned to Laura, who was busy looking toward Cole with concern in her eyes. "Let's do it. At least we might be able to have some small comfort of a bath and bed tonight. Laura, Cole is pressing this very fast and I am worried about that. It's like he wants to find those responsible right away and do them in. That is not like Cole. Is there something that we two can do to quell those feelings?"

"I've felt them too, Johanna. After dinner, I'll speak with him. I have only seen him like this once before. It was when I was shot from behind by a crazed rancher. Cole killed all five men responsible. It took him a good while to shake it off and realize that his real calling was the law and being U.S. Marshal. You know that he has ridden some long and very lonely trails—sometimes after some very hard and vicious men. He has faced off with several that I can name and they were all evil men."

"Yes, Laura, I know that. It was him that taught me to read my instincts when it came to shooting."

"He did the same for me, Johanna. Cole somehow knows in the back of his mind when there is danger, and he waits for it. Maybe that is the key, Johanna. Maybe, just maybe, he fears for our safety, not his. After all, the Dakotas are a wild place, and he is the lone protector of two women. Or, could we just be hampering him? Protector? Hell, we two can take care of ourselves. Let's you and I do our own investigating into this matter. Come the morning, you and I will dress up a mite and ask some questions—among the womenfolk. We might even be able to solve this situation very quickly."

"I agree, Laura. Let's do everything that we can do as women to help."

* *

Cole Stockton stepped into the jailhouse and stood silently appraising the two men who occupied chairs around the single desk for a long moment.

Tom Kolbert looked up with a wide grin on his face.

"Can I help you, mister? You seem lost. I'm the Town Marshal and this man sitting here next to me is the County Sheriff. We are the *Law* hereabouts."

Both men's grins suddenly turned grim when the tall lanky man standing before them cast them a silent glare, reached into his inside vest pocket and pinned on the silver star of a United States Marshal.

They looked into the piercing blue-green eyes and John Ranger swallowed hard. The man wasn't smiling.

"I'm Cole Stockton, U.S. Marshal. Firstly, I want to speak with Deputy U.S. Marshal Merrick, secondly; I want both your badges on the desk."

"Well, Marshal—that is, iffen you are who you say you are, Deputy Merrick just up and left. He just ain't around no more."

Both men grinned with ugly sneers.

"That is NOT what I asked you. I want to speak to Deputy Merrick. Where is he?"

Kolbert spoke up, "He is probably down at the Chinese Opium House. He's an Opium drunk, you know. He is known for his wildly shouted threats and illusions. Yes, you can find him there. Ask for Chin Ly Lau. He will show you your friend."

"Thank you," replied Stockton. "Now, take off those badges and place them on the desk top. Then, you can get yourselves out of this jail and never look back."

"By whose authority? You can't do this. We are the law here."

"Correction! You WERE the law. I AM THE LAW and my authority is *Samuel Colt.* You have three seconds to drop your badges or I will personally rip them off your shirt fronts. One-Two-Thr..."

"O.K., Marshal Stockton. We will humor you. But, when the Town Committee hears of this, they will demand your dismissal and our re-instatement. Then, where will you be? Think about that, Marshal."

"Send them on over here. I'd like nothing better. As far as you two are concerned, you had better pray to the Almighty that I never get dismissed. Because if I do, I will hunt you down and kill you where I find you. I will leave your dead carcasses for the scavengers of nature to take care of. Do YOU understand ME?"

Tom Kolbert didn't like it one bit. This man stepped into HIS office, just looked at him and John Ranger and told them to drop their badges on the desk. He was going to protest when he glanced at John Ranger. Ranger was already unpinning his Sheriff's star and the look on his face was one of sheer FEAR.

Kolbert turned his glance to look directly into the eyes of U.S. Marshal Cole Stockton. He slowly reached up and unpinned the Town Marshal star and laid it gently on the desktop. He had looked deep into the eyes of Cole Stockton and saw his own soul burning in the fires of Hell.

He knew then that if he protested in anger or even touched his gun, he would never live to see another day. Cole Stockton was legendary, yet the man to take him would have the reputation of Top Gun of the West. Tom quickly erased that thought from his mind. Wealth and Power was his motive, and his friends would see that he retained both. His friends would put him back in power once again.

Both of the newly renounced lawmen left the office and headed to the Eureka Saloon. They would appraise Nate Osborne of the recent developments, and Nate would not be happy. This newly arrived Marshal would die, or at least be put out of action real quick. Nate was a man of action. He would immediately send for someone to deal with this man Stockton, and ultimately, his wounded brother and the Deputy that they kept drugged with opium in the Chinese Sector.

Nate Osborne listened to his two *appointed* lawmen with ever increasing fear. Clay Stockton was one thing. They had at least succeeded in rendering him unable to function for a while. Sandy Merrick? They merely drugged his morning coffee at the local café, then, smuggled his limp body through back alleys to the Chinese Sector where Nate paid a goodly sum to keep the man under sedation—turning him into a ghostly apparition of what used to be a man, begging for more opium.

Cole Stockton was another problem. This man was ruthless in his pursuit of justice. Nate looked deep into each man's eyes and saw the fear that resided therein.

"You two are cowards! There ain't no man on the face of this earth can look into a man's soul—except the *Devil* hisself. No man can do that. You two are just plain ole cowards. Get out of my sight. Go up to the Canadian ranch and work with the boys up there. I will take care of Mr. Marshal Cole Stockton. I have just the right man in town to do it. Yes, I think that Marshal Stockton should meet Jacques. Yes. Jacques Le Fevre hates lawmen, especially U.S. Marshals. I'll arrange a meeting, perhaps this very night."

* *

Cole Stockton carefully read the jail log book, then, took the keys and went back into the cell block. He asked each prisoner his name and what charge that he was arrested for. He released six out of ten of the inmates, their crimes were just misdemeanors. He told them to go home.

To the remaining four prisoners, he leaned back against the log wall and rolled a cigarette. Producing a match, he lit it, then took a long puff and let the smoke slowly blow out and encircle his head.

The four prisoners moved to the front bars of each cell. They smelled the sweet aroma of tobacco, something each had not had for many days. They slowly inhaled the aroma while watching Cole Stockton with curious eyes. This man wore the star of a Marshal, but did not act like any Marshal they had ever seen before. This man knew what stirred the senses of a condemned man. They searched his eyes for long moments, and he found the Devil within each of their souls. They understood and nodded.

Stockton slowly walked from cell to cell and unlocked each. He stepped back and pulled the makings from his vest pocket. He set them in the center of the dirt floor, along with one match. He backed against the log wall and grinned a silly grin. The cell doors opened almost as one, and the four prisoners stepped out into the open.

The first man out was big. He was French and stood almost six foot three with solid muscle. The second man was short, but wiry. He had a sneaky look to his eyes, but they glowed with relief. The third man was smooth. He stepped out of the cell with fluid movement. He was well dressed. His hands were soft and well used to the good life of slicking a hand or two of poker.

The fourth man was also a big man. He emerged slowly from the cell, always watching Stockton's eyes. This man was a cold- blooded killer wanted by many states.

Sean Killabrew looked straight into Cole Stockton's eyes and nodded. Killabrew knew Stockton from a few years previous down in the New Mexico Territory. He knew exactly what Stockton was capable of and would do, if provoked. Sean wanted to live. He was also curious about what Cole had in mind for them.

"And what do we have here this fine day, Cole Stockton, U.S. Marshal? Mr. Stockton, what do ye want of us poor condemned souls? Those of us that are sentenced to die would gladly have you shoot us between the eyes, rather than face *the rope*. Is that why you are here, Mr. Stockton, to shoot us between the eyes?"

"No, Sean, I am here to see justice, and I need good Deputies. I figure to Deputize all four of you."

Frenchy spoke first, "What makes you think that we will make good Deputies? After all, there are two of us in here for murder. The other two of us are in here for grand theft. How are you, the Marshal, going to justify us as Deputies?"

"First of all, I think that we all understand each other. I don't like the local law here and I just relieved them of their badges, illegally, of course, but they had NO CHOICE, and your choice is no choice. You will serve as my Deputies or I will lock you back up and see to your hanging—a bit early maybe, like in the morning. I hate to prolong the obvious, but I have a job to do, and it doesn't entail nursing the likes of you four. Now, the job is open, take it, or get hung first thing in the morning. Let me know by sunrise of your decision."

Their Decisions didn't take long. It was a chorus of voices, "Marshal, we'll take the job."

"Good! First one of you that quits without authority from me, I'll hunt down and kill. That's a promise. Raise your right hand and repeat after me, "I...do solemnly swear that I will uphold the laws of the Constitution and of the United States of America, so help me God."

Each man swore his oath, and Cole Stockton pinned a Deputy U.S. Marshal badge on each man. They looked appraisingly at each other

46

and wondered at what they had just done. No one could have predicted this turn of events.

Stockton then handed each man a gunbelt and revolver.

"Load them and put them on. I want you to walk around town and become known for what you are—Deputy Marshals. Any person that gives you trouble, you use whatever force necessary to bring this person to me. I will deal with the situation. Right now, Frenchy, you are in charge. I have two ladies that I must meet for dinner. I'll be back after that. See to it that you four are seen by a lot of townspeople."

* *

Clay Stockton lay napping in the bed when he sensed, rather than heard the door to his hospital room softly open and close. He listened, keeping his eyes closed and senses open to sounds.

Momentarily, the light scent of a familiar perfume wafted softly on the air, and then, a soft hand touched his. He immediately knew who it was.

He opened his groggy eyes to behold his mother, Johanna's smiling face looking at him. He gathered a returning smile and squeezed her hand. They stayed like that, not speaking, for several long minutes.

The door opened again and Cole and Laura entered the room. Just knowing his mother, Cole, and Laura arrived, Clay was filled with a sense of reassurance that he would heal quickly and be on his feet within a relatively short time. The four talked briefly and then Johanna and Laura departed. Clay kept Cole at his bedside and told his story.

It was around one hour later that five men, all wearing silver stars denoting Federal Marshals, descended upon the Chinese Sector of town and with *gentle* persuasion, mainly the darkened bore of a Colt Revolver, managed to produce one drugged up Deputy U.S. Marshal Sandy Merrick.

The five Marshals escorted Merrick to the hospital floor of the hotel where he was placed in a bed opposite Clay Stockton. Sid Henderson, the sneaky-eyed Deputy sat in a chair just outside the door, a double barreled shotgun across his lap.

Clay grinned against the dullness in his brain and thought,

"Yup, he's only been here a few hours and already the fats in the fire. He is churning that urn so fast that no one can figure what's on his mind. My God, he's even got convicted killers as Deputy U.S. Marshals. What next? I'll bet that he is going to send that *Frenchy* feller up to Canada to scout into those gold mining activities. Why the hell didn't I think of that? Frenchy knows the people, he's on the run, he can ask questions and be harbored like a fugitive. But, will it work? Will Frenchy honor his *appointment* as Deputy Marshal?"

CHAPTER NINE

"The Ladies Are Tasked"

Cole, Johanna, and Laura finished their supper at the Bismarck Restaurant and stepped out into the street. They had just turned toward their hotel when a loud boisterous voice blurted out "Hey! you there! Yah, you! You, with the shiny star on your vest! I am Jacques LeFevre and I don't like you. I don't like any United States lawmen. I think that I will kill you right here and now!"

Cole looked toward the stout, long haired Frenchman with the hate twisted face and long scar down his left cheek. He motioned the two women away from him.

"So, how are you going to kill me? By boring me to death with your brash talk?"

"Cole!" Laura exclaimed "He's got a shotgun!"

"Yah, I know. You two move further away."

Laura and Johanna moved cautiously back ten more feet.

"I'm going to cut you in half with buckshot, Mr. Marshal. Then, I'm going to blow your head off."

"That's bold talk for a DEAD MAN. By the way, you are under arrest for threatening a Federal Marshal."

"The Hell you say!"

LeFevre whipped the shotgun up to his shoulder with his thumb cocking back both hammers. His eyes were wild with excitement.

Cole Stockton's right hand blurred to his holster and the deadly Colt lifted smoothly out and leveled straight at LeFevre's chest. The Colt bucked in Stockton's hand and in the next instant he was fanning the hammer back and squeezing the trigger again.

LeFevre jerked back with the impact of the first lead. The shotgun rose into the air with both barrels discharging at once.

LeFevre's eyes went wide and his mouth dropped open. An ugly red stain was spreading across his massive chest.

LeFevre had seen the draw and couldn't believe it. This man standing before him should be dead, but he was like greased lightning and hot molten lead beat Jacques to the punch. The second and third slugs took LeFevre close to the first and the fourth round smacked into his face. LeFevre fell straight back to lay in a pool of blood with unseeing eyes staring into the face of Hades.

Stockton opened the loading gate of his Colt and punched out four spent rounds. He reloaded four fresh ones and slowly walked up to the twitching body of Jacques LeFevre.

A crowd had gathered and they stood quietly watching the Marshal. Other Deputy Marshals now stood around the area watching the crowd's faces. The undertaker arrived and took charge of the body.

One person in the crowd of spectators didn't like it. Nate Osbourne grimaced. His best killer had underestimated this man Stockton and now he was stone cold dead. Nate now had second thoughts. It would take more than one man to take out any Stockton. He pondered on this fact with cold steely eyes.

* *

Cole escorted Johanna and Laura to the hotel and then went to the jail to give last minute assignments to his *Deputies*.

Johanna and Laura were softly talking in Laura's room when a gentle knock came at the door. Both women drew revolvers and then Laura said, "Who is it?"

An unmistakable feminine voice shakily replied, "A friend. Please hurry and let me in."

Laura cracked the door. It was Marcie Sweet, one of the Eureka Saloon girls. She was extremely nervous and glanced back over her shoulder, peering down the hallway. She quickly stepped into the room and the door was shut behind her.

50

The three women moved to the far corner of the room and sat at the small table. Marcie spoke in very soft, almost inaudible tones "I came here because I know you are with that new Marshal. I was passing by Nate Osborne's office earlier, and overheard him speaking with Tom Kolbert and John Ranger. Your Marshal friend had just run them out of the jail and they were furious. Nate told them to go up to Canada and work on some kind of ranch. They left about two hours ago. Nate is also the one who arranged for Jacques LeFevre to kill your Marshal."

Marcie stopped speaking for a long minute, seemingly listening for any sound outside the room in the hallway. Finally, she felt safe in continuing "I've known about stolen Canadian gold and some killings for about three months. Up until now, I have been too scared to tell anyone. Nate would kill me if he found out. He would kill any of us girls if we told anyone about the gold. I want out of Bismarck, but am afraid that Nate would kill me if I tried to run."

Again, Marcie listened for hallway sounds.

"I saw the gunfight between your Marshal and Jacques, and that gave me the courage to come here. I know now that there are lawmen who aren't afraid of this gold smuggling ring and want to break it up. I decided to help anyway I could. Please pass this information to your Marshal and also—please, don't tell anyone where you got the information. I'd better go now."

Laura and Johanna hugged the young brown-haired girl who had risked so much to help them and squeezed her hands for reassurance. Laura opened the door and after checking both ends of the hallway, let Marcie out. She quickly disappeared within the dim shadows of the hallway.

"Well, now", said Johanna "Imagine that. Now we have some information for Cole. See, I knew that we women could find out things that a man couldn't."

A quick rap at the door announced that Cole was back and Laura let him into the room. Johanna and Laura explained about Marcie's hushed visit. Cole pondered the new information for a few moments.

"I'm going over to the jail again. I'll be back in about an hour."

Cole entered the jail and assigned Frenchy the detail of catching up with and following the two dismissed lawmen into Canada.

"Frenchy, I want you follow those guys and watch every move they make for this next week. I want to know where they stay, who they talk to, where they ride to, and what they do all day and all night long. I want to know everything there is to know about that ranch they are headed for. Can you handle that?"

"Oui, yes, Marshal, I can handle that. Don't worry, I'll be back in a week with all the details."

"Good. Now give me back that badge. I don't want anyone to find it on you should you get yourself in a situation. You'll have to talk your way out of it, or rely on your own wits to get back here safely."

"I understand," Frenchy nodded. "I'll be back. I kind of like being on the good side for a change. Besides, I never did like those two."

Cole turned to Sean Killabrew. "O.K. Sean, you are in charge now when I'm not here. Keep a close eye on the town. Come to the hotel and get me, if anything strange happens—don't try and handle it yourself."

Cole then strode back to the hotel and gathered up Laura and Johanna once again.

"Well, ladies," he began, "get a GOOD night's sleep, because I have a chore for you to do tomorrow night. You will be taking a long ride and camping out in the wilderness for a few days."

"Just what do you mean by a long ride, Cole?" asked Johanna.

"I want you to STEAL, Naw, rather, I want you two ladies to CONFISCATE a herd of horses and mules from the Rocking Cross Ranch and drive them towards the Black Hills. I am going to up the ante in this deadly poker game, and right now, I am betting that I hold the high hand. Rest well, ladies. Goodnight for now. I'll have more details in the morning."

Cole bowed slightly, then went out into the night to ponder his next move. Both women stood there, mouths open and wide-eyed.

"Listen to him—a United States Marshal, and he wants us to STEAL a herd of horses and mules. Has he lost his senses?"

"No, Johanna. It makes sense. He, rather, WE are going to take away the transportation method of the stolen gold from Canada. That will really make these guys riled up, and will instill distrust from the Canadian faction. They'll balk at trying to deliver more gold to their meeting place, and that gives the North-West Mounted Police more time to locate them when they try to move it. Not only that, there will probably be bad feelings all throughout the smuggling ring and then someone will make a big mistake. That's when Cole and Clay, if he is up and around then, can prove who all is in this thing, and round them all up. Yes, Johanna, it makes a lot of sense to me."

"Now that you put it that way, it does sound like a good idea. Well, we wanted to help. There it is. I'll see you in the morning, Laura."

CHAPTER TEN

"Setting the Stage for Justice"

Early the next morning Cole Stockton checked on his brother Clay and Deputy Merrick. Merrick was awake and although he still shook with the aftermath of opium wearing off, he was in good spirits. In fact, he wanted to get out of bed, get his gun, and go shoot it out with a few SOB's that drugged his coffee.

Cole and Clay both laughed. The doctor and his wife had given remarkably good care to both men. Clay was feeling much better and was on the verge of climbing out of bed himself, but Cole cautioned him to stay in bed and rest some more. He handed both men their gunbelts and told them to keep them handy. Although he had Sid Henderson and James "Slick Jim" Eaton alternating guard outside the door with a shotgun, he felt better that both men inside were armed. Besides, if any trouble started at the hospital, the guard could enter the room and then there would be three guns to reckon with.

Cole recounted to Clay what actions he had taken so far, and Clay just shook his head and chuckled. Sandy was grinning from ear to ear. Cole Stockton was a man of action all right—just the kind of action that Sandy liked.

"By the way, Cole, Sandy knows an old Indian that might be able to help us. He is Lakota and comes from the Black Hills. We can get him and a few of his friends to watch out for Johanna and Laura. I'd feel better about that. Of course, we don't want to tell the women; they might refuse the help."

"That sounds just fine. Sandy, how do I get in touch with this old Indian?"

Cole left the hospital with instructions on how to contact the old Lakota, *Runs His Ponies*. He would take a ride a little later in the day. He next went to the hotel in time to join Laura and Johanna for breakfast and coffee.

Cole watched the clientele as he sipped his coffee. He took note of the features and eyes of every man in the restaurant. A couple of men tried to avoid his eyes. These were the ones that he concentrated on the most and when they lifted their eyes again, they found him looking right into the mirror of their souls. They shuddered as an icy chill surged through their bodies. Two of the three men suddenly got up and left. The third stood his ground and stared back at Cole Stockton. Cole put on that knowing grin and nodded slightly. This made the third man uneasy. Stockton knew what he was there for—to watch his every move and report it to Nate Osborne.

Stockton suddenly stood up and walked straight up to the man.

"Tell Osborne that I had three eggs, sausage, biscuits, and coffee for breakfast. If he wants any more information, tell him to come and see me himself. Now get out before I lose my sunny disposition."

The man slowly got to his feet, hands kept deliberately away from his gun, and backed out of the restaurant.

"Well now, how about some more of that good coffee?" Cole motioned the waitress over with the pot.

The waitress spoke softly while filling their cups. "Your brother Clay was doing the best he could, but I'm glad to see he's got some help. It's nice to finally see some quick action against those bullies. They think that they own the town of Bismarck, but there are good citizens here who want a safe and peaceful place to live. I think that our dream is fast coming, thanks to you and your Marshals."

"Well, Miss, give us a few more days and you'll have your town back. My word on it."

The waitress smiled warmly as she turned and went about serving other customers.

* *

Nate Osborne was furious. Cole Stockton had spotted his men and had run them out of the restaurant. He had even invited him to come and see him for himself. Osborne knew what that meant. If he wasn't man enough to face Stockton by himself, then don't send your boys to do a man's work. He had issued the challenge.

Osborne had to do something now, or lose face with his own men. He had ridden roughshod over them and they believed that he was tough. Osborne was deadly with a Colt. Everyone knew that, but Stockton was LETHAL. Sweat beads formed on Osborne's forehead as he contemplated his answer to Stockton's challenge.

* *

Cole rode out of Bismarck in the early afternoon. Nate Osborne watched him go from the window of his upstairs saloon office, while one of his gunmen stood in the middle of the room, awaiting orders. He wondered where Stockton was going. Should he get some of his boys and try to regain control of the town? He observed Sean Killabrew step out of the jail and take a chair by the door. As long as Killabrew and those hard cases were deputized, there could be no open daylight moves.

Nate spoke, "I think that we'll start our play tonight. We'll start with the hospital. There is only one guard there. He should be easy to take, and then, I'll personally take care of that botched job on Marshal Clay Stockton and that loud-mouthed Deputy of his. After that, I'll wait for Cole Stockton and take care of him—for all time."

Osborne turned to one of his henchmen with a question, "Is Kyle Starbuck still out at the Ranch?"

"Yeah, Boss. He's just itching to get into a scrap with one or both of them Stockton boys."

Starbuck was a notorious gunman from Montana. It was he who had done much of Nate Osborne's bidding when it came to cold-blooded out and out killing. Starbuck stood five foot eight, was slender, and next to Osborne, the fastest gun in the outlaw ring. Neither Starbuck nor Osborne held any remorse for their deeds.

"Good. Send for him. Tell him to come into town the back way and meet me here at ten o'clock. We will pay a visit to the Stockton's that they will never forget."

* *

Meanwhile, Cole rode slowly into the Lakota camp. All eyes were on him. He held his right hand high, away from his guns, to indicate a peaceful visit.

He was able to single out *Runs His Ponies* by the description that Sandy gave him, and he rode straight up to him and waited for the invitation to dismount.

Runs His Ponies nodded, and Cole Stockton dismounted and exchanged pleasantries. They entered a large animal skinned Tee Pee and seated themselves around the small fire. Runs His Ponies looked into Cole Stockton's eyes and read them.

"Why does the Mar-shal come to *Runs His Ponies?*"

"I have need of your skills. Marshal Sandy has been hurt and my brother Clay Stockton has been shot, but lives. I need help to bring the evil men to justice."

Cole waited a few seconds as he read the interest in the Lakota's eyes. "There may be much danger in it, and there might also be many ponies to be taken—much like the old days. Are you interested?"

"This is strange. Why does the white Mar-shall want the Lakota to have such fun?"

"There are many bad white men who steal the yellow iron from the Great Northland and I must stop them. My mother and woman will take many ponies and mules from these bad men tonight and drive them into the Black Hills. I want you to do nothing more than to watch out for them. Keep them from harm. Should some bad men follow this herd, my women will fight them. Should they need help, I want you and some young men to help them. I will see that you are rewarded with many ponies if you do this. I will turn my back and you can take as many ponies as you need. There will be no white men to complain. This is my word."

"I shall do as you ask. Mar-shal Sandy is a good man and I see the honor of your words in your eyes. You are a man of many battles and honor. I am honored that you come to *Runs His Ponies* for help. We will do this."

They smoked the pipe and had a Lakota elk stew with wild scallions. Cole left the camp with a good feeling in his heart. Johanna and Laura would be silently watched and protected while they carried out his wacky scheme.

* *

It was nearing nine o'clock in the evening when Cole Stockton, Johanna, and Laura left the livery stable and trotted out of town. Sean Killabrew and Sid Henderson strode through town together, making their nightly patrol for trouble. Slick Jim sat outside the hospital door with the double barreled shotgun across his lap.

Inside the room, Clay Stockton suddenly turned to Sandy and announced, "Sandy, I've got an itch crawling up the back of my neck like there is something about to happen and I can't shake it. I think that all hell is going to break loose this very night, and I think that it is going to start right here in this room. We'd better keep them Colts handy."

"Well, Clay, I wasn't going to mention it, but the hairs on the back of my neck are prickling up. That's a sure sign that trouble is on its feet and headed our direction. You are damn right that we will be ready. I'm just itching to do something."

The two Marshals called Slick Jim into the room and spoke in low tones. They agreed on their plan of action.

* *

Cole, Johanna, and Laura slowly worked their way through the darkness to the Rocking Cross Ranch. All was quiet as they approached the main ranch buildings with its adjoining holding pens and grazing pasture for the special herd of twenty-five horses and twelve mules.

Cautiously, they approached the rear of the barn and stable area. Cole dismounted and, drawing his Winchester, looked at both women.

He had that silly grin on his face. His eyes were lit up like a young boy about to partake in mischievous frolic.

"The herd that we want is in the grazing pasture next to the stables. I'll give you two exactly fifteen minutes to drop the bars on that fence and start them horses and mules milling. After that I'm going to start a ruckus. I always wanted to shoot up an outlaw rancher's castle, and now I got my chance. Just get those animals and head south toward the Black Hills. I'll take care of the fun part. One more thing—don't look back, just keep going as fast as you can."

Laura and Johanna nodded and turned their horses, Mickey and Brandy, toward the pasture area. They looped their ropes around two fence posts, and then with a mighty tug from both horses, the section creaked—then, popped.

The entire fence section slammed to the ground. The startled animals nervously milled around and suddenly trotted toward the open country-side.

Laura galloped to the front of the herd leading them southward. Johanna took up the rear driving them forward. Within minutes the horse and mule herd disappeared into the darkness toward the Black Hills.

No sooner than the women had gone with the herd that Winchester Rifle fire erupted. The two women heard the sharp cracks being systematically fired. That rifle fire was answered within seconds from over a dozen revolvers and other rifles. The firing was fairly intense, but they could still identify the steady cracking of Cole's Winchester.

Both women let out a loud Comanche war cry, and flapped and waved their lariats all around. The entire herd broke into a fast run toward the south. They rode fast and hard until they could no longer hear the crackling of gunfire. After the run of a few miles, the animals tired and slowed to a steady walk. It was a long way to the Black Hills, a little over three hundred miles.

* *

Cole was having a great time. He levered round after round into the downstairs windows. In fact, he was out to smash them all on his side of the house. He even fired through the upstairs windows—aiming high in case there might be innocent women and children in those rooms.

As anticipated, there was a sudden response of heavy revolver fire from the first floor windows. Stockton watched the bunkhouse to the left, and every so often would throw a few rounds that way. The answering fire from those darkened windows was minimal. That told Stockton that he had caught the main party inside the ranch house.

"Probably holding a meeting on when and how they are bringing in the next shipment," thought Cole. "Well, they are going to have a slight delay."

* *

Glenn Turnbull was indeed conducting a meeting with his most trusted men. He was outlining the plans for their next foray into Canada.

"One million dollars in gold," said Turnbull, and you could see the glint in every man's eyes.

"We'll leave at daylight. We'll take the usual precautions—four pack trains, only one will have the gold shipment. The Mounties will play hell trying to figure out and chase down which one has the payload."

Suddenly, the conversation was interrupted by smashing glass in the window; hot lead whistled across the room, and imbedded itself in the far wall. All occupants immediately flung themselves to the floor, and drew their revolvers among surprised expletives.

Men crawled across the floor, working themselves to the window sills. They saw periodic bright orange stabs of flame and fired directly at them. The thundering flames were in one place, then another. It was almost like there were five men firing at them from across the yard.

Glass was shattering all over the house. Glenn Turnbull was loudly cursing the men who were ruining his home. At one point, he actually stood up and shouted his challenge, "You somebitch, you don't know who you are dealing with. I will find kill you for this."

A bullet whizzed past Turnbull's left ear, and two of his men grabbed him, jerking him to the floor. The rolling thunder of rifle fire suddenly stopped. A *deadly silence* followed.

Turnbull waited until he could wait no more. He heaved himself upright and stood in the wake of his damaged living room. Glass was lying everywhere. Favorite paintings, artifacts, and his wife's precious statue collections were shattered to pieces. Lucky for him, she was not home. Large darkened holes and spreading cracks glared at him where the heavy 44.40 rounds smacked into the walls.

Turnbull was furious. Who would dare to do this to HIS house? His furor increased two fold when one of his wranglers from the bunk house stormed into the room and announced, "Boss—someone has made off with our entire herd of special horses and pack mules."

"That does it!" screamed Turnbull, almost shrilly. "Get mounted. We will track down those that did this, and they will pay with their very lives. A thousand dollars goes to the man who finds them. Three thousand dollars goes to the man who kills them."

* *

Cole Stockton had his fun. He grinned from ear to ear as he suddenly stopped firing and mounted Warrior. He rode off into the night, toward the south. He would trail Johanna and Laura for a few hours, just to confuse any trackers while they attempted to follow the trail of the missing herd.

Cole rode for an hour, then pulled Warrior off the trail, up into a blind of bushes at the top of a knoll. He withdrew his Winchester and waited. He waited for over an hour. Just as he was about to mount and ride for Bismarck, he heard the slight click of a horseshoe against rock. He readied himself, Winchester at the ready.

Mylan Gorn, one of Turnbull's men, was bent over in the saddle and intently watching the trail of several hoof prints when the sudden thud across the back of his head bowled him over the saddle and he hit hard on the ground. Cole Stockton wasted no bullet on a tracker, he just silently came up behind him and laid a rifle barrel across his skull. Stockton grinned that satisfied grin again. One tracker down, and maybe a couple more to go.

* *

Laura Sumner and Johanna Stockton drove the herd as fast as possible through the night. At one point, Johanna rode up to Laura and exclaimed, "I can't put my finger on it, but I feel that we are being watched. It is almost the same feeling I had back in the days of the Comanche raids. The hairs on the back of my neck are standing straight up."

Laura replied, "I thought that I was the only one with those feelings. I have felt that we were being watched very closely for several miles now, too. Still, I've seen nothing nor anyone to validate these feelings. Johanna, I have complete faith in Cole, and I trust him with my life, but this is absolutely WILD. I have never dreamed that one day, I would be RUSTLING a herd of horses and mules from some rancher because a U.S. Marshal told me to do it."

* *

Sunrise found Cole Stockton seated beside a small fire making coffee. Surrounding him were three trussed up men from the Rocking Cross Ranch. Cole grinned at them as he poured his morning coffee. A sudden slight disturbance bothered the horses. Cole looked to Warrior. His ears were pricked up and he stamped as if in contempt of something.

Cole backed away from the fire, his coffee cup still in his hand. He eased the Colt in his holster a bit as he moved back away from the fire. Although it was dawn, it was still gray enough to hide figures in the shadows. A voice slowly drawled from his left side, "Howdy the camp! I seen your fire, and could shore use a cup of fresh coffee. I been traveling all night up from Colorado and New Mexico way."

"Come on in and sit a while, have some coffee," replied Cole.

The lone figure stepped into view, leading his dun horse. He was a middle-aged man, standing six feet at least. He wore two guns, tied down, in the manner of a knowing gunfighter. His flashing brown eyes and reddish hair set him apart from the crowd. He held a ready smile, and Cole recognized him immediately.

"Rance Turkley! You are a long way from Texas. I won't ask you how you left, I can guess."

The tied up men exchanged glances of disappointment. This gunman was a friend of Stockton.

"Cole Stockton! Fancy meeting you up here in the Dakotas. I'll tell you no lies. You know how I left Texas. You can figure the whys and wherefores', one step ahead of the Rangers. I ain't wanted north of Texas, and I see that you are wearing a U.S. Marshal star. You figure to take me?" Rance took in the scene around the fire.

"Not that I couldn't, Rance, but I'm not in the mood for that right now. I have other fish to fry. Mind your manners and we'll share some coffee, jerky, and biscuits."

"I'll take your word, Cole. You have my word. Peace between us for right now. Say, I notice that you have some other guests at your fire. While I'm in the area, might I offer my assistance?"

"W-e-l-l, O.K., but, remember, I didn't ask you. There may be some ill-mannered hombres on my back trail. They'd be looking for some missing animals. To tell the truth, Rance, I've rustled some stock, and these guys are nasty, mean to the bone. I could use a bit of help."

"There is nothing like old friendships, Cole. Let's give any takers a welcome they won't easily forget. Besides, I need a bit of fun since them Rangers chased me out of north Texas."

Cole Stockton and Rance Turkley! Two of the fastest and deadliest guns in the Southwest sat together drinking fresh campfire coffee, and chawing on tough beef jerky and cold biscuits. There was a mutual understanding between them. The three trussed up figures lay quietly listening to the two gunfighters. They wanted NO part of what was to come.

CHAPTER ELEVEN

"A Royal Flush"

Kyle Starbuck rode in from Turnbull's Ranch, dismounted, and tied his black horse up behind the Eureka Saloon. He stepped confidently to the back door and was surprised to find a guard there. Once recognized, he was immediately let into the back offices of the saloon.

Starbuck stood in front of Nate Osborne, "I got the word and I'm ready for action. Just why the hell did you hire those two losers off the street? I could have taken Clay Stockton face to face, and that deputy of his, too. You just don't have enough confidence in me, Nate. Why, I can even take YOU."

Osborne scowled back at him. "You have never seen the day that you could come close to me, let alone Stockton. Now we got a bigger problem. Clay Stockton is FAST, but now his brother, Cole Stockton, is in town. I can take Clay myself, but its Cole that I'm worried about. He's got the reputation. I don't think that any man alive can take Cole Stockton face to face."

"Well, Boss, I guess that we will have to do the old *you face the man, and I'll cover from behind, just to make sure trick*. It hasn't failed us yet."

"We will get to that. Right now, you and I will take care of three lawmen. There's a Deputy that sits outside a hospital room. Clay Stockton, as well as that loud-mouthed Deputy Marshal of his are inside. We'll go within the hour. Go have a drink or two at the bar, on me. When we get back, we'll celebrate the killing of three lawmen and look forward to the killing of Cole Stockton next."

An hour later, the two men crept stealthily up the back stairway of the Bismarck Hotel to the hospital floor. Both men held the foremost thought in mind that tonight, they would finally kill Clay Stockton and his Deputy.

The two men stepped up into the foyer. Osborne eased around the corner. The guard, Slim Jim, suddenly stood up, stretched a mite, then entered the room where Clay Stockton and Deputy Marshal Sandy Merrick lay in recovery.

The two men drew revolvers and stepped softly to the targeted room. Nate put his ear to the door. He listened carefully but heard no sound. He shrugged, then motioned to Kyle. They both cocked their revolvers, and then, Nate kicked the door open.

Both men dashed into the room, revolvers blazing. Hot lead flew everywhere, and an otherwise quiet night in Bismarck, North Dakota was shattered by the quick cracking of Colt Revolvers and an intermittent shotgun blast.

Osborne entered the room and stepped immediately to the right. Starbuck leaped into the room, Colt blazing, but he never knew what hit him. In one instant, Nate and Kyle were thundering their Colts, and in the next instant, a trio of weapons cracked and boomed, sending a hailstorm of hot molten lead into their bodies.

Osborne jerked with the ugly thud of not fewer than seven well-aimed Colt .44 slugs to his body. Kyle suffered the full blast of an aimed Express shotgun at point blank range. His body slammed back against the opposite wall as a myriad of heavy buckshot tore his body virtually in half. Kyle slid down the wall; an ugly red smear marked the path of his descent to the floor.

Clay Stockton emerged from behind the crudely erected barricade to survey the damage. They had thrown up both beds on end, all the furniture that they could move into place, and hunkered down behind this wall of sorts when the door suddenly burst open and two wild men jumped into the room firing their revolvers at where the beds used to be. The lawmen suddenly stood up and fired their weapons directly into the intruders. Every round hit exactly where aimed.

"Damn!" exclaimed Sandy, "it sure makes me feel good to empty my gun into an SOB like Osborne. It was he that arranged all of our misery. The other feller, I recognize from the Canadian *Wanted Posters*."

Sandy waited a moment before continuing, "Clay, both of our feelings were right. Yet, someone is missing. I want that scum, Kolbert. He is the one that arranged the drugging of my morning coffee, and besides, he thinks that he can take me."

"Well, Sandy, I feel like getting out of this here room, and reading the law to a few people! How do you feel about that?"

"Right, Clay! Let's smoke out a few others. I'm ready to settle some scores and—and..."

"Settle down, Sandy. I think that we've evened the score for a bit. Let's just stroll down to the restaurant and have breakfast like men. I can almost taste those buckwheat cakes sopping with maple syrup, fried eggs, bacon, and biscuits."

Clay turned to Slim Jim. "Jim, you hang on here. I'll send the undertaker up to clean up this mess. Come back to the jail when they are finished here." Slim Jim acknowledged his duty. He could hardly wait to tell anyone who would listen about what a fight he had just witnessed.

* *

"Frenchy" Charboneau followed his prey into Canada. He silently watched them from ridges, hilltops, around the corners of buildings, and from the far end of the bar in the most notorious saloon in the small Canadian town.

Frenchy was so engrossed in his task that he failed to notice two North-West Mounted Police approach him from behind. Within seconds, Frenchy was handcuffed and led away to the jail. He kept his silence, for the time being.

Frenchy was wanted for murder in Canada and one of the assigned Mounties matched his face together from old wanted posters in a desk drawer. Several hours later, the Mounties led in another prisoner, John Ranger.

Ranger had gotten drunk, very drunk. He babbled on into the night, and Frenchy memorized each and every word.

Frenchy contemplated this turn of events. He had to break jail and he couldn't do it alone. He had to have some help, from where, he knew not.

Frenchy called the jailer, Jonas, to him and asked for a pencil and paper. The jailer handed both to him through the bars. Frenchy wrote out a telegram and asked the old timer Jonas to send it for him. The jailer's eyes grew wide with recognition at the addressee, Cole Stockton, Bismarck, North Dakota.

Jonas Wharton had not seen nor heard the name "Cole Stockton" in the last twenty years, but he well remembered the fair-haired, blue-eyed, slender kid with the fast gun that had saved his bacon during a saloon shoot out with half a dozen hard-cased hombres in Las Vegas, New Mexico. Jonas was in his prime then and the town's marshal at that time. He went into the Silver Slipper Saloon to arrest one man, called Johnny Rocco, and found himself suddenly surrounded by a gang of six. He knew then that his life was numbered in seconds.

From out of nowhere, a soft voice came behind the gang members and suddenly, the entire saloon was thundering with death and destruction. The slender, blonde-haired young man just up and drew two Colt Revolvers and started shooting the gang members where they stood. His draw was like a blur and the sting of lead was deadly.

Within moments, half of the gang lay dead or wounded on the floor. The others all crouched with hands held high. Johnny Rocco among them. The young stranger stood ready with cocked Colt and determined grin.

"You can take your man now, Marshal. I don't think that anyone else will object."

"What is your name, Son?"

"For whatever it's worth, I'm Cole Stockton. Just glad I could help out, Marshal."

When all was over, the young man finished his beer, mounted his dun horse, and rode out of town. Jonas wondered about this man, yet there were no *Wanted Posters* on him.

A thought flashed across Jonas' mind, "Someday, I hoped to repay him for saving my life."

Now, Jonas in his late sixties had moved to Canada, and found work as jailer in the Mountie controlled town. Jonas read the telegram once again. He looked Frenchy straight in the eyes and read his soul. Frenchy looked deeply back at him and then nodded his understanding as Jonas slipped the document inside his shirt front.

Jonas waited until his shift was over, then he wandered down to the nearest saloon. He partook of his evening shot of whiskey with beer chaser, then touching his shirt front, ambled out of the saloon and down the street to the telegraph office. He stood outside the door pondering a bit. He glanced at the message once again, and finally made his decision. He entered the telegraph office and sent the message as written with understanding with the telegraph operator that the contents could not be shared.

Jonas stepped outside the telegraph office and looked into the evening sky. Stars were beginning to twinkle and the moon seemed to shine even brighter than he could ever remember. He felt good for the first time in a long while. He felt like he had finally repaid a long time debt.

* *

Laura Sumner and Johanna Stockton sat uneasily around their small campfire. The small herd that they were *escorting* was no particular problem. Still, both women had the distinct feeling that their every move was being watched, and watched very intently.

They finished their meager supper of sliced beef, roasted potatoes, and canned tomatoes with biscuits and then moved back from the glow of the campfire. They both had learned this rule from their wise fathers and husband. Only a novice would sit in front of a fire, letting the glow of flames or coals brighten their eyes. A true camper of the wilderness moves back from the fire and accustoms to the darkness. Danger could come from the darkness at any time, not from the fire.

* *

Runs His Ponies and twenty Lakota warriors ringed the two women that night and lay silent among the elements of nature. No two white women in the entire Northwestern Territory had such protection as they did.

"No harm will befall these women." spoke *Runs His Ponies* early on to his warriors. "They are blood relatives to a great warrior of many battles and plenty coups. I have given the Lakota word. We shall abide by the word of our ancestors. We shall honor our word for the justice that this warrior seeks."

* *

Cole Stockton and Rance Turkley lay on their stomachs facing the direction from whence the trackers had come. Both men had read the eyes of the trussed up men and knew exactly where the main body of pursuers were. A knowing look into the north during the night showed the glimmer of campfires.

The rancher's men were only a matter of an hour or so distant from them, and when the two factions met, the Devil would have his dues.

The rest of the riders advanced cautiously, having heard nothing from any of the three trackers that went before them. They spread out with Boss Rancher Glen Turnbull riding in the lead.

Turnbull was MAD. He was CONFIDENT. He was the OLD HE BULL of the Territory. He would catch those rustlers and hang every last one of them.

"Shall we?" came the soft voice.

"Why the Hell not? Let's do it Cole."

Two men suddenly stood up on a knoll in front of the twenty ranch riders. Both men held rifles at the ready.

One man called out, "Well, now. You must be Glen Turnbull and the Rocking Cross riders. Sure glad you brought a lot of help, Turnbull, because you're going to need it. I am Cole Stockton, United States Marshal, and you and all of your men are under arrest for murder, theft, trafficking in stolen gold, smuggling, and whatever else I can think of. Please, let me add resisting arrest to that. You can come peaceably, or over your saddles, and it won't make any difference to us."

Turnbull grinned crookedly. There were only two men standing in front of him and he had twenty men to back him up.

"The Hell you say! We will ride right over your dead and broken bodies. Get them, Boys!"

The scene that followed was one of sheer catastrophe, for the rancher, that is. He and all of his men drew their weapons at the same time.

Flame and hot lead belched from the muzzles of two Winchester Rifles. Horses reared, bucked, sun-fished, and threw their riders to the ground as heavy rifle lead flew through the air. The sharp thunder resounded again and again as bright orange flame spit death and destruction. One by one, rancher men fell to the well-aimed methodical fire of the two lone men on the knoll.

Within ten minutes, a third of Turnbull's men were dead or wounded, and neither of the two men on the knoll had been touched by frantic return fire. Turnbull's men anxiously looked to their boss for guidance. Turnbull glared even more viciously. He shook with rage, his eyes wild beyond all comprehension.

"Rush them, men! Kill them both! We can do it! There are only two of them!"

Three men rushed forward and were immediately cut down by well-aimed Winchester fire. A few men attempted to reach their mounts. Those who mounted were allowed to leave with their lives.

An uneasy silence hung over the tense scene. Several minutes later, Cole Stockton walked warily down the knoll and confronted Glen Turnbull face to face. Turnbull just sat there on the ground, his revolver held limply in his hand and a dumbfounded, bewildered look carved upon his bearded face. How did only two men shoot hell out of his trained force of twenty riders?

"Turnbull, you and all your men are under arrest. Drop that pistola or take lead. You are finished in this territory."

Turnbull looked up at Cole Stockton with unbelieving eyes. His men had been shot to pieces with precise accuracy, and he still couldn't believe it. He limply held his pistol out to Stockton. It slipped off his fingers to thud to the ground. His eyes glazed over with sheer wonder and utter defeat. He realized he was lucky just to be alive.

Stockton stepped to the side and picked up the dropped revolver. He produced a set of handcuffs and secured the now demure rancher's hands behind his back.

Rance ambled down the knoll and helped Cole provide aid to those who needed it. When all had been settled, Cole suddenly turned to Rance. His hand held a cocked revolver. Rance's eyes grew wide with surprise, and fear. Was Stockton arresting him, too?

"Raise your right hand and repeat after me." Stockton ordered his helper.

A few minutes later, Rance Turkley, wanted man and known gunfighter, stood in awe at what had just happened. He glanced down at his shirt front and couldn't take his eyes off the Silver Star that adorned his chest. He had been commandeered as a Deputy U.S. Marshal to *escort* prisoners to jail. He couldn't believe it! He was wearing the star of peace. It was unethical. He looked into Cole Stockton's eyes. The man wasn't kidding.

Stockton stood grinning that fun-loving grin of his and knowing that there was no better person to escort these people to jail. As for himself, he had a chore to finish. He needed to catch up to that herd to do it. Rance would escort the prisoners to Clay at Bismarck.

* *

Tommy Ryan, the telegraph runner, strode into the Iron Griddle cafe and found Clay Stockton and Sandy Merrick enjoying their first good breakfast in well over a week.

"Marshal Stockton, I got this here telegram for your brother Cole, but I figured that you might want to see it."

Clay took the telegram and read it. It was the message from Frenchy.

To: US MARSHAL COLE STOCKTON, BISMARK, ND. STOP. TRAILED QUARRY. SHIPMENT FROM NORTH RANCH ARRANGED

FOR MIDNIGHT MAY 2. STOP.
KOLBERT AND RANGER TO ESCORT. STOP.
NORTH CONTACT IS STILLWALL. STOP.
JAILED BY NWMP. HELP. URGENT. STOP.
FRENCHY.

Clay wasted no time. "Tommy, wait a minute. I want to send a reply right away."

He took the runner's pencil and wrote out a return message addressed to the North-West Mounted Police Headquarters.

"Send this right away, Tommy."

"Yes, Sir!" and the kid dashed out the door.

Clay turned to his Deputy, "Well, Sandy, would you be up to taking a long ride towards the North? It seems that Kolbert and Ranger are coming back here. I think I know just about where they will cross the border at and I also think that we should greet them. Especially, since they will be carrying stolen gold with them."

Sandy smiled at the prospect, "That suits me to a tee, Boss. When do we leave?"

"Tonight, but first, we are going to pay a visit to Banker Grant. I want no leak from this side of the border as to what has transpired in the past few hours. We are going to break this case wide open and within twenty-four hours I expect all hell to break loose. I have already notified the North-West Mounted Police of the Canadian contact and they are watching his movements. We will be the welcoming party on this side of the border."

* *

Frenchy sat alone in the cell block of the jail. He was bored. He sorely wished that he was out on his own and free in the wilderness. He missed the forest and the sigh of the wind through the pine boughs. He thought to himself, "If I, Frenchy, get out of this mess, I will go straight and live right, so help me, God."

The cell block door suddenly opened and NWMP Corporal Jarvis stepped up to the cell door. He unlocked it and swung the heavy iron door wide open. He was smiling.

"Come, Frenchy. You are free to go. You have some friends waiting for you in the outer office."

Frenchy could hardly believe his ears! What friends could this be?" A sudden nagging feeling that all was not right flashed across his mind. He hesitated at the door to the cell block. He turned slightly to see that Jarvis had drawn his pistol and held it at his side. What was about to happen?

Frenchy swallowed hard. He turned back toward the cell block door, then suddenly rammed himself backward into the surprised corporal.

The pistol flew to the far end of the cell block as Frenchy and the corporal grappled in a life and death struggle.

Jarvis was a big man, stocky, weighing over two hundred pounds, and standing six foot four against Frenchy's six foot three muscular frame. They were evenly matched as they traded hard blows to the body and face.

Frenchy threw a quick right cross, but Jarvis side rolled and, catching Frenchy's arm, threw him off balance and into the iron bars. Jarvis began choking the life out of Frenchy when the cell block door opened and a slim figure stepped into the dimness.

Frenchy tightened his neck muscles against the iron bars in an effort to resist the murderous pressure applied by Jarvis.

"You die, Frenchman! You'll not live to tell another tale!"

One moment Jarvis was slowly choking the life out of Frenchy: the next moment he grunted with the hard thud of a revolver barrel across his skull.

Jarvis slumped limply to the floor, releasing his hold on Frenchy, who immediately also fell to the floor, gasping for breath.

Frenchy looked up wide-eyed into the eyes of his savior. There stood Jonas Wharton. The old jailer grinned like the cat that swallowed the canary.

"Ole Jarvis was tough, huh. Always wanted to smack him one and now that he is found out, we done got us a prisoner. The NWMP will be glad to know that we have caught us one of the gold smuggling ring amongst their own. I guess the plan was to shoot you in the back while you were supposedly breaking jail."

Frenchy was finally able to speak, roughly.

"You saved my life, Jonas. How can I repay you?"

"Well, Son, I guess for the time being, I am the only semblance of a lawman here in this town. Inspector Wilkes from NWMP Headquarters is on his way here. He telegraphed ahead and directed arrangements for the arrest of some Canadian factions, and for your release based on word from C. Stockton, U.S. Marshal. That's how Jarvis knew about you being with the law. I just happened to be in the telegraph office and saw the message copy. I run over here as fast as I could. Anyways, I need you to stick around and help me with this turncoat Mountie until the Inspector arrives. You can sort of be my deputy jailer."

Both Frenchy and Jonas laughed.

"All right, Boss. We—that is, you and I—the Frenchman and the Old Man are the law in this jail until the Inspector arrives. Let's lock thees tyrant up before he comes to and we both have to fight him." Jonas nodded with a chuckle.

* *

It was near noon when Cole Stockton caught up to Laura Sumner and Johanna with the herd of horses and mules. They were relieved to see him and waited eagerly to hear what was next.

"O.K. Lady Deputies, let's ride back to Bismarck," stated Cole with a smile across his face.

"What about the herd, Cole? Shouldn't we be driving them back to Bismarck also?" Laura was completely confused about the situation.

"No, Laura. I have a special posse that will take good care of this herd. Just leave them as they are."

Both women looked at each other and shrugged. There was no posse in sight, but Cole's confidence convinced them. The three of them turned and rode slowly toward Bismarck.

At that time both Johanna and Laura felt the hairs on the backs of their necks prick up. They looked back over their shoulders.

Their eyes went wide as they observed about twenty Lakota Sioux warriors appear out of nowhere and begin gathering up the herd.

Just ahead of them, Cole rode easy in the saddle with that silly grin spread across his face. He chuckled to himself and then began to whistle a lively tune.

* *

Banker Grant was just closing the doors of the Bismarck Bank when two Federal Marshals pushed the doors open again.

"John Grant. You are under arrest for theft and conspiracy to ship smuggled stolen gold. You can come peaceably or feet first. It don't make any difference to us."

Grant looked deep into the steeled eyes of Clay Stockton and raised his arms above his head. He had nothing to say.

"Cuff him, Sandy. I guess he don't want no part of gunplay. I've never met a banker that did. They like to hire it done, though."

* *

Clay and Sandy had just finished locking the cell door on Banker John Grant when they heard a call from outside the jail. They strode to the door, opened it, and stepped out into the street. Sean Killabrew was headed toward them from across the street.

Rance Turkley sat his horse in front of the jail with his entourage of cuffed, tied up, slumped over-wounded, and over the saddle dead riders.

Clay Stockton looked at the Deputy Star on Turkley's shirt front and just shook his head. Once again, Cole had gone hog wild making Deputies. This time, he had deputized a known and wanted gunfighter on the run.

"Hello, Clay. Cole said to deliver this group to you. I don't think you'll have any more trouble from the likes of these boys. They put up quite a struggle, but between Cole and me, we changed their minds about not surrendering."

"Thanks, Rance. Sean, Sandy, help Rance get these guys inside and lock them up. I'll send for the undertaker for the others."

Glen Turnbull was sullen and almost lifeless when they helped him down from his mount and escorted him into the cell block.

Sandy commented, "Clay, this here jail is filling up mighty fast. Why, we've got more visitors here than I've seen in a coon's age." Sandy then turned to the prisoners, "Sit back and relax boys, you ain't going nowhere for a long time."

* *

In pitch dark the eight mule pack train wound its way through the maze of rocky ground and pine forest. Tom Kolbert was in the lead and John Ranger brought up the rear of the pack train. Each two mules were led by mounted packers. They traveled as silently as they could.

Kolbert finally caught sight of the clearing he sought. When they reached the other side of the clearing, they would be in the United States, North Dakota to be exact, and only one hundred or so miles to Bismarck.

He grinned with the thought that this was the shipment to make him rich. He and the others would escort this smuggled stolen gold to Bismarck, have it hidden in a wagon, and then drive it south toward Mexico. A man could live a life of luxury in Mexico with that kind of backing.

The pack train was half way across the clearing when a dozen riders suddenly appeared on their back trail.

"Mounties!" yelled John Ranger as he whipped his horse into a gallop.

It was now a race for freedom and wealth. The mules broke into a fast run. Gunfire erupted into the night as the pursuing NWMP surged forward. Bright orange blossoms of fire flashed in the darkness and deadly hot lead sought out victims.

One of the packers suddenly threw up his arms and jerked off his horse. His mules balked and jerked sideways to veer towards the right. They slowed to a walk and suddenly stopped, looking as stubborn as ever.

John Ranger felt the burn of Winchester lead as it creased his waist. He yelped out and slumped in the saddle, but kept his balance and continued to race toward the United States side of the clearing.

A second packer went down within the hail of bullets. His mules also slowed and mingled around before stopping. Four laden mules would not deliver their precious ore.

Tom Kolbert pulled up sharply, circled his mount, and yelled encouragement to John Ranger and the remaining packers.

"Come on, only a few short yards to go. Bring them mules, steady now, don't look back. Keep them packers coming."

He drew his Winchester and returned fire at the Mounties. John Ranger pulled up beside him and, drawing his revolver, also fired a few rounds at the pursuers.

Both men turned again as one and sunk spur to their horses. They watched the six remaining pack mules cross into the trees at the far side of the clearing.

"We got six mules loaded with gold. We're still rich," yelled Kolbert. John Ranger silently slumped forward against his horse's neck, but held on.

The two disgraced lawmen made it to the trees at the far end of the clearing. They stopped and looked back. The Mounties had stopped. They weren't coming any further.

"We did it!" exclaimed Kolbert.

They rode into the trees to find the packers and mules standing in a group. The packers had their hands held high in the air. Five federal Marshals sat their horses in front of them, revolvers drawn.

Kolbert went wild-eyed with surprise.

"Howdy, Tom," drawled out Sandy Merrick "We've been waiting fer ya. Raise your hands and come peaceably or drag iron."

Kolbert snarled as his hand flashed for his Colt. He was going to finally kill that loud-mouthed Deputy Marshal.

His revolver just cleared the holster when Merrick's Colt exploded with fire and hot lead. The first bullet took Kolbert straight in the chest and the second thudded close to the first. Kolbert slammed backward off his mount to lay grotesque in death. His widened, disbelieving eyes staring lifelessly into the dark sky.

John Ranger tried to raise his hands, and fell limply to the ground. He had taken two more Mountie rifle bullets in the back, but he was still alive. He would live to stand trial.

Sandy Merrick holstered his Colt. "Well, Clay. I think that this situation is over. Between them Mounties and us, we got everyone involved in this smuggling ring. A clean sweep of the pot as they say in poker—a regular Royal Flush."

* *

Two days later a group of *unlikely companions* sat around a long picnic table. The group included Clay Stockton, Cole Stockton, Laura Sumner, Johanna Stockton, Sandy Merrick, Frenchy Charboneu, Sean Killabrew, Rance Turkley, Slim Jim, and Sid Henderson. They told stories, joked, and just generally dug into the passel of fried chicken, cobbed corn, beans, and corn bread. Afterwards, chocolate cake finished off the meal. There was lots of good hot black coffee.

Johanna Stockton had announced to her family first that morning that she would stay in Bismarck and visit with Clay for a while. Laura and Cole would ride back to the Lower Colorado together. The two looked into each other's eyes and everyone at the table could see the precious love that passed between them. Johanna looked at Clay Stockton and winked. Clay nodded back to her, an approving grin spreading across his face.

CHAPTER TWELVE

"The Journey Home"

In late spring of 1879, our latest adventure had brought us to Bismarck, North Dakota Territory where my younger brother Clay is the U.S. Marshal.

Laura saddled up our horses, Warrior and Mickey, while I readied our packhorse for the long trip back to the Lower Colorado. Mother, who accompanied Laura and me to Montana and subsequently to Bismarck, decided to stay on and visit with Clay for a while longer.

When we were ready, Laura and I led our horses and pack animal to the Iron Griddle Cafe where Johanna, Clay, and a few new friends were waiting breakfast and to see us off.

We looped the reins over the hitching post and entered the café to find our friends waiting at a long table with red and white checkered tablecloth. As soon as we sat down, platters arrived heaped with crisp bacon, steak, fried eggs, and hotcakes were set in the middle of the table. On the side sat maple syrup, biscuits, fresh butter, honey, and lots of that good hot black coffee.

Breakfast was hearty and would sustain us for most of the day on the trail. Finally, all of our friends stood around us outside while we swung up into the saddle.

Mother looked up at us, "Cole, Laura. You take care now. It's a long way back to Colorado. Write us when you get back. Tell us about the trip."

Laura replied, "We will, Johanna. Wire us when you get ready to come back. We'll be looking for you."

We waved to them, turned our horses and trotted out of town

toward the Montana Territory. Montana was a wild place in the late 1870's and dangers were abundant. There were renegade Indians, sudden storms, unfriendly wildlife, and the possibility of highwaymen such as thieves and murderers. We rode easy in the saddle, avoiding ridges and continuously scanning the landscape for signs of danger.

The scenery was beautiful. We rode through thick forests of pine and spruce, up and down hills of tall grasses, through fields of fresh scented wildflowers, around steep rocky ledges, up crude rocky paths, and down through wild ravines.

We crossed several small streams where the water was clear and cold. Trout were abundant and with the first evening's camp, I rigged a makeshift pole, and while Laura set up our camp and got a small fire started, I caught us four beautiful trout for our supper.

We camped in a clump of pines that dissipated any smoke from the small glowing fire so as to not attract outlaws or Indians. After supper, we sat back a bit from the fire, listening to the sounds of the night.

We sat there together, watching the big sky and feeling the warmth between us. Everything seemed right. I turned to Laura and read her eyes. She lifted her face to me and the kiss that followed could have started a forest fire.

We were finally alone after several weeks on the trails and we spoke our thoughts to each other. We didn't say much. We didn't have to. We could look into each other's eyes and know what the other was thinking.

Finally, we rolled up in our blankets and I placed one of my Colt Revolvers close to hand, under the blanket. That was a fact of life for me now. My hand was never too far away from that Colt.

* *

Morning began with slight lighting in the east. The air was fresh and smelled of pine and wildflowers. A bit of dew moistened the land during the night and there was a slight chill in the air.

I slipped out of my blankets and set about adding tinder to our still smoldering campfire coals. Within a few minutes, I added a few dried branches. After the flames licked about hungry for fuel, I added a few pieces of kindling for a cooking fire.

I stepped quickly down to the stream and filled our coffee pot with icy cold water and, once it was boiling, tossed in a handful of Arbuckle's coffee. Momentarily, I had trail biscuits warming and a small skillet with beans and bacon.

Laura slowly moved in her blankets, stretched, and opened her eyes. She inhaled the savory aromas of our trail breakfast and through wisps of tussled hair hanging down in her bleary eyes, she seemed to come alive to the day.

"Come on, Sleepy Head, its daylight, time to pack up and travel some more."

Laura crawled out from her blankets, yawned, stretched, sat down and pulled on her boots, then stepped over to the fire where I handed her a cup of steaming hot coffee. She smiled as she sipped the dark liquid.

After our hot breakfast, I saddled the horses and arranged the pack horse while Laura washed up the breakfast dishes and utensils.

Once repacked, we were ready to resume our journey. I poured the last of the coffee over the smoldering coals, and then covered it with dirt. After about a quarter of an hour, we put boot to stirrup and swung into the saddle.

Today's travel would take us through some of the wildest country ever traveled by man. We rode with a close eye on the horizon, the weather, and our back trail. We had not planned to visit too many towns on this trip, but to mainly enjoy the wilderness. I felt peace with myself out in the wilds, and as we rode, Laura could sense a oneness with nature also.

Laura smiled to herself as recollection of her old Uncle Jesse's words came to mind. "Well, there ain't nothing out there in the wilds twix you and God, but yur own self and the elements of nature." Uncle Jesse was right. She loved the trails.

After several miles, I was in the lead and we were riding between two small grassy hills. Warrior's ears suddenly pricked up, so I pulled up short and motioned for Laura to stop.

I listened for a long moment, then pointed to the ground beside me. Laura moved forward, and dismounted. I did the same, while drawing my Winchester.

I whispered for Laura to stay put and then crouched down and made way to the top of the incline.

After a long moment, I motioned for Laura to join me but to stay low. She ground hitched our horses and tied the pack horse to Warrior's saddle horn. She moved quickly and silently up the incline to lie face down beside me.

I silently pointed ahead. There they were. At least twelve fiercely painted renegade Sioux Warriors riding across our line of travel.

I pondered the situation before speaking in low tones, "Laura, you can look at them, but don't stare. If any look this way, avert your eyes immediately. Those that ride the wilds can sense danger and they will know that someone watches them."

Suddenly, one, a Warrior with blackened face and white stripes zig-zagged like lightning bolts, turned and looked straight at us. Laura closed her eyes.

After several minutes I reached over and gently touched her cheek. She relaxed.

"You're trembling," I said "Just take a deep breath and relax. Breathe easy. They will pass shortly. We will wait for a spell, then be on our way again. Laura, I know what you saw, but don't let it bother you. I gave him a good look and he sensed it—I think he feels the sacred bones of his ancestors. That's a bad omen to an Indian—to be visited by the dead."

It's been said by some that hardened gunfighters can look into the eyes of those that they face, and see souls burning in the very fires of Hell. I'd heard that about me, but I disregarded those stories as old codger trail tales.

Half an hour later, we once again swung up into the saddle and headed south. Out of habit, I suppose, stopped for a long moment and studied the hoof prints left by the warrior band.

Laura watched me for a moment before remarking, "Cole. If you want to backtrack for a while, we can do that. I mean, if you have a feeling that someone might need help, we can go."

Well, she knew me pretty well. "Thanks, Laura, I was just thinking. I've always back tracked parties such as this for at least a few miles. Sometimes it's nothing, but, then again, I have had to bury some hapless folks."

"Let's follow your hunch, Cole. Your feelings are usually right."

We turned to the west and followed the Indian back trail for an hour. We saw nothing out of the ordinary and started to turn back toward the south.

Suddenly, all three horses pricked up their ears and the pack horse was reluctant to move further. I once again drew my Winchester.

"Wait here, Laura."

I rode slowly forward to an area of thick bushes, my eyes searching here and there, taking in everything. I cocked my head a bit and listened. Warrior suddenly shied and stepped back.

I dismounted and moved to the thicket on foot. I entered the dense, thick, and tangled foliage.

Laura drew her Colt .38, and stood ready. Mickey was nervous and she spoke softly to him. He settled as soon as she spoke.

I reappeared out of the thicket, and walked to the pack horse to withdraw our small shovel.

"Laura, take the horses up about thirty yards and turn right into the thicket. There is a small clearing there. We'll make camp here tonight. Go ahead and unpack, I have a chore to do."

She knew what that meant. Someone, rather, what was left of someone, needed burying. She did as I bid and began to set up a camp for the night.

Finally, I finished my chore and thrashed my way through the underbrush to step into the small clearing. I was sweat-streaked and dirty. I held my tongue and didn't say anything about my findings. There was no reason to alarm her further.

I could feel Laura watching me for a while. I remained quite silent. She looked deep into my eyes and for just an instant, I believe she thought she saw the torment of a fiery soul in hell. Just as quick, it was gone, and a look of softness filtered across my face.

I stepped up to her, gently took her hand and looked deep into her eyes. She felt the penetrating power of my mind and suddenly felt loved and secure. She wrapped her arms around me, and could almost swear that she felt a slight shiver run through my body as I held her close.

We had a <u>very low</u> fire that night and right after supper, we moved back from the coals to lean against the base of some large pines. We kept our Winchesters with us, close to hand. We sat together like before, but tonight it felt different. We intently listened to sounds of the night.

Laura finally drifted off to sleep, and I gently placed a blanket around her. Later, told me she dreamed of home, her ranch, her wranglers, her horses, and her best friend lying next to her.

CHAPTER THIRTEEN

"Poor Family Wagons"

Cole and Laura continued toward the south once again. They watched for signs of nature and were rewarded with several sightings. Cole spotted an eagle diving toward a stream and pointed it out. They saw deer, a few buffalo, an elk, and some red fox.

They crossed some more creeks and could see the dark outline of fish lying among the reeds in mossy nooks along the shoreline. White water splashed over rocks in the streams and made the unmistakable sound of babbling. Everything seemed so peaceful.

About forty miles from their last camp and traveling half way up a mountain slope parallel to a small valley, they saw the wagons. There were two wagons, and by the looks of them, a most ramshackle outfit. Laura had seen better horseflesh sold for dog food. The small bunch of cattle trailing the wagons looked stringy and worn as well.

Cole motioned a halt and Laura rode up beside him. He remarked, "Looks like some more poor colored families looking for the Promised Land."

"You've seen the likes of this before, Cole?"

"Yes, Laura. I've seen a lot more now-a-days than in times previous. These folks come from points south, expecting to find a bit of land where they can raise a family and be left alone to work their small patch of land. The biggest problem is that most of the good land is filled with cattle, or lands that are sacred to the Indian. They try to settle down, only to be run off by some rancher and his riders. Some of them aren't so lucky. I've buried a few in my travels."

"What do you want to do, Cole?"

"Well, I was thinking. Let's ride down there and introduce ourselves. They might even have some coffee, or we could share ours. Follow my lead."

The traveling duo rode right down the side of the mountain and angled toward the wagons. They rode slowly and were able to take in the entire scope of these people. It was as poor a sight as either had ever seen. There were two families with about five or six children each and they were ragtag.

They rode within hailing distance. Cole waved his hat into the air and shouted out, "Hello the wagons. We are traveling south. Can we join you?"

The people looked at the newcomers for a few moments, and then one of them, a man, waved for them to come forward. As they approached the wagons, they were studied closely. Cole could see the suspicion on their faces when they saw that Laura was wearing a gun belt also. Some of the children had the look of fear and Laura wondered about what had frightened them before.

The wagons stopped and the two elements made introductions. A noon meal was mentioned and the women and a couple of older girls began to build a small fire and prepare some food. Their rations looked mighty meager for people traveling in the wilderness.

"Cole," Laura whispered, "we have so much and these people have so little. Let's give them some extras." He nodded his approval.

Suddenly, Laura was surrounded by four little girls in tattered dresses. They appeared fascinated by her outfit of boots, jeans, chaps, dark blue shirt, yellow bandanna, dark rumpled jacket. Most of all they wondered about the gun strapped around her slim waist.

Mickey seemed intrigued and reached out his neck to the girls who stroked him quickly, then pulled their hands away. Laura laughed a bit. "Go ahead and pet him. He won't hurt you, he likes that."

The children stepped closer to Mickey and he just stood there soaking in all that attention. Laura smiled.

Within half an hour the distinct aroma of a fine stew and fresh ground coffee floated in the air. Cole and the three men were talking in low tones and Laura sensed an aura of urgency.

Cole finally walked back over to her, "Laura, there may be some trouble. It seems that these people left their homesteads one jump ahead of some ranchers and their riders. They suspect that they may be followed and harm done. I intend to stand here and read the law to whoever might come upon these people."

"Am I still deputized?"

"Damn, did I forget to release you from your oath?"

"Yes, Cole. As it stands right now, I am a Provisional Deputy U.S. Marshal. I guess that I have to stand ready with you."

That familiar grin spread from ear to ear as Cole chuckled quite audibly. "All right, Laura. But, I want you behind some cover and ready with that Winchester to back me up. I will be right out in the open. I want the boss man himself. Maybe, just maybe, we can forgo any bloodshed. I certainly hope so."

The travelers were right in the middle of their noon meal when a distant dust cloud caught their attention. Cole studied it for a few moments, "Laura, take your Winchester and get over behind the left wagon. Cover that side."

Cole sat there with the people and continued eating his stew and sipping his coffee.

The dust cloud formed into a dozen riders, all grim faced, hard-looking men. A big man of about six foot one led them. The riders spread out as they came, drawing rifles and holding them at the ready.

Cole Stockton exhaled a bit, set his plate down and stood up.

The rancher and riders rode straight up to the camp. They looked at Cole and sneered.

The rancher spoke, "Seeing as you are a white man, you got one minute to fork your bronc and light out. After that, I figure you for one of them and will shoot or hang you right along with them."

"Is that a fact? I think that's bold talk from a dead man."

"Just who the Hell do you think you are, Mister. I got a dozen riders here and I don't like you."

Cole never flinched, "You got that part right, and you ain't going to like the rest of it one bit either."

A real cocky young man wearing a fancy pair of revolvers edged his dark brown horse up to the spokesman.

"Boss, this guy wears his gun like he is some kind of gunfighter or something. Bet I can take him. Let me handle this—besides it will be a show that them colored people won't forget. Let me kill him for you."

"All right, Lenny. Show this meddler what a real Montana gunfighter is."

Sitting back in the shadows of the wagon, Laura just shook her head. This young fool didn't know who he was facing. Cole just stood there while this man dismounted and faced him.

The kid grinned at Cole and then made a big mistake. He stared right into Stockton's eyes. A long moment passed and Laura saw the kid's hand tremble slightly. She held her breath.

The kid was sweating. She could almost feel it. He looked at Cole and said, "What name shall we put on the marker, Mister?"

"Well, you can put LENNY MILLER for a start, and we'll sort the others out later."

The leader suddenly caught the jest of what was happening.

"Just who the Devil are you?"

Cole reached into his vest pocket and pinned on the Silver Star,

"Cole Stockton, United States Marshal. You can drop your gun belts or drag iron, it don't make much difference to me or to my Deputy."

You could have heard a pin drop in that camp. No one said anything for a long minute.

Laura stepped out from behind the wagon with Winchester leveled at the three left most riders.

"Damn! a woman Deputy. I never seen the likes of this."

Cole stirred up the pot a bit more. "Rest assured that she will fill you with lead, should you not drop your guns. O.K., Lenny, are you ready? Want to drag iron and die, or do you want to drop your fancy guns in the dirt?"

Lenny looked up at his boss. His mind was already decided.

"Take him, Lenny!"

"Take him yourself, Mr. Larson. I KNOW who Cole Stockton is."

Joel Larson looked pale as all twelve of his riders unbuckled and dropped their gun belts to the ground. Cole stood there with that winning grin on his face.

"Well, Larson?"

Joel Larson turned white as a sheet, but likewise unbuckled his gun belt and let it drop.

"All right. One man stays here for an hour. He will bring your guns with him. The rest of you start back to wherever you came from. Should I hear of ANY of you harassing these people again, I will hunt you down and shoot you where I find you. Do I make myself clear?"

They all agreed and rode out except for Lenny Miller. He was elected to carry all their guns to them. For the next hour, Lenny followed Cole all over the camp. After he left, the wagon people crowded around Cole and Laura.

"Suh, we ain't never seen the likes of this. You is a good man and we thanks you for it. We'd be proud to have you join our group and travel with us for long as you want."

Cole and Laura rode with them for the next two days, and then the wagons turned toward the West. They waved farewell to the people with the wagons and continued southward toward the Lower Colorado.

* *

It was early afternoon on the fourth day of travel that they passed within a few miles of the Little Big Horn. It was just three years earlier that General Custer and five troops of the Seventh Cavalry had fought their last battle. Although not within sight of the scene, Laura had a sad eerie feeling—like they were being watched by hundreds of eyes.

Cole seemed not to mind, but he was quite silent for a long hour. Three times they ran across groups of tracks—unshod ponies, and each time Cole studied the tracks. Within minutes he could tell how many were in the group, how fast they were going, what the ponies were feeding on, and just about how long previous the band had ridden through the area.

"This kind of backs up my thoughts, Laura. A lot of people believe that ALL of the Sioux and Cheyenne ran to Canada after the Little

Big Horn. These trails tell a different story. There seems to be small parties of Indians moving toward the Yellowstone. There could be trouble brewing."

Laura had to agree with Cole. They continued to ride ever vigilant to sound and sight.

Twenty miles later they camped just inside the Wyoming Territory. The land for the most part was open rolling hills. They found a campsite next to a small creek and settled down for the night. It also was a cold camp as they didn't want any fire to advertise themselves to those who may be lurking within the area. This was still the land of the Cheyenne and Lakota Sioux.

Morning came softly from the east and once again, Laura woke to find Cole watching her. She smiled, "Don't you ever sleep?"

"Oh, I get four or five hours. That seems to be enough to keep me on my toes."

After a meager breakfast of dried beef jerky, cold biscuits, and water, they saddled up and once again continued southward.

They had gone but ten miles or so, when they spotted the dust cloud. They halted and watched it grow into a stagecoach and six horse team.

They angled toward it and within twenty minutes were sitting easy on the road watching the coach boil to a sliding stop. Dust flew everywhere and they could hear a couple of passengers coughing.

The stagecoach driver couldn't believe his good luck. He knew these riders. "Well, I'll be doggoned. Cole Stockton and Laura Sumner! Fancy meeting you two way up here in Wyoming. Ya'll on vacation or something?"

"Hi Ya, Sammy! No, we're just traveling back to the ranch and saw your dust cloud. We thought that we might ride along with you a bit."

"I'd like that, Cole. Sure could use the company. Jeb, here, my shotgun guard ain't the best when it comes to jawing and telling good stories."

Jeb felt no disrespect. He had ridden shotgun before and knew Sammy always liked to tease him.

"Aw, come on now, Sammy. Didn't I tell you those two real good whoppers?"

"Yah, Jeb, about a hundred miles ago. Beats me why I let you come along in the first place. You ain't my favorite shotgun, you know."

Now, the back and forth took on the rhythm of an often repeated good natured conversation.

"Yah, and I know why. I don't let you talk my ears off. Besides that, I let you know right off to your face that you are a cantankerous old buzzard. No competent shotgun guard in his right mind would ride with you. I must've been crazy with the fever when I accepted this run."

Sammy turned to his friends on horseback. "See what I mean, Cole, Laura? Listen to what I have to put up with—all the way to the Lower Colorado. Say, by the way, how is that lovely lady Johanna doing? I sure liked her makeup. I hope to meet up with her again, soon."

"Well, Sammy. You just might. Johanna is up in Bismarck right now, but I suspect that she will be coming back our way within a month or so. She might just ride your coach again."

"Now that would be mighty pleasant. I'd much rather have her up here on the high box, than the present company."

Cole and Laura couldn't help but laugh. These two, for all their picking at each other, were good friends. Jeb Wilson had ridden shotgun on and off with Sammy Colter for the past ten years. They knew each other very well and trusted each other with their lives.

"O.K. Sammy, we'll ride alongside and chat a bit. We might even stay overnight at the next rest stop, providing the food is decent."

"In that case, Cole, you might as well keep on riding. There ain't a station on this here route that has what I would call good food. Well, the coffee is decent enough."

Sammy chuckled loudly as he relayed those thoughts. Jeb just nodded his concurrence.

Sammy slapped the reins to his team, "All right youse cayuse rebates, let's stretch into that harness. Come on now, Bessy, show them studs how to pull this coach. He Yaw, get up there!"

Cole and Laura trotted alongside the coach and traded conversation with Sammy and Jeb. The ride was most pleasant.

Laura thought to herself as they rode, "I was glad that we are going to stop at the overnight station. A real bed would be nice after a week of sleeping out on the ground. Besides, a nice hot bath would feel real good. A lady has got to indulge herself with at least a bit of luxury now and then."

Ten miles later found Cole and Laura dismounting, unsaddling and turning their horses into the holding corrals at the stagecoach overnight station.

The aroma of simmering stew, fresh baked biscuits, and fresh ground coffee floated enticingly on the soft evening air currents. Cole and Laura looked at each other and knew that they would feast tonight. Anything was in preference to cold jerky, biscuits and water.

After supper, Laura paid the station mistress to draw her a bath and took a nice hot soak with softly scented soap. She relaxed in the water for at least half an hour. After dressing in some lady like clothes, namely a riding skirt and blouse, she and Cole sat on the front steps of the station house and watched the stars. It was very peaceful.

Close to midnight, Laura went inside to a bunk and Cole stayed out on the porch to chat and smoke with the boys.

She must've been more tired than she thought, for as soon as her head hit the pillow, she was drifting off into a world of dreams.

She envisioned she and Cole standing in a multi-colored meadow of wildflowers. He had his arms around her and they were looking into each other's eyes. She felt at peace with the world and the sun was shining its warmth down upon them. Laura smiled in her sleep and snuggled closer to the pillow.

CHAPTER FOURTEEN

"The Overnight Coach Station"

At dawn with pouring rain in every direction, Cole Stockton stepped out on the corner of the porch of the stagecoach way station and pondered, "The West, being what it is, never ceases to surprise me. These early morning thunder storms won't allow us to travel for a while. We might as well make the best of it. We'll have to wait it out just like the rest of the coach passengers."

He hesitated before continuing his thoughts, "I am just as glad that we stayed the night in the overnight station. I sure would hate for Laura and me to have been caught out in this storm. The Lord takes care of those who heed his signs."

Cole turned back inside the building to look over the hearty breakfast as the station cook wrangled up mountains of hotcakes, fried eggs, steak strips, biscuits, fried potatoes, country gravy, and lots of hot black fresh coffee.

One of the two women passengers, to earn her breakfast for free, volunteered to serve the tables. She was rather good at it, and may have been a waitress before beginning her travels westward. She was smiling and having a good time, and all the passengers and other patrons appreciated her friendliness.

Laura thought to herself, "Mother always said that the way to a good man's heart was to cook him a meal that he would never forget. I've seen some pretty homely girls proposed to because of the mouth-drooling meals that they were capable of. A lot of real pretty girls felt really frustrated and without close men friends because they couldn't cook worth a damn."

She thought more about herself, "I guess that I am a pretty fair cook myself. All of my wranglers have stayed on during lean times, and all that they asked was for me to cook them their favorite dish. Problem was, they never told me what it was. I just cooked whatever came to mind and they devoured every bite of it."

She smiled a bit while she reminisced of days past, "During holiday seasons, my wranglers made any excuse they could think of to visit the main ranch house and sneak a cookie or cinnamon roll or two when they thought I wasn't looking. In fact, all my wranglers are like *little boys* when it comes to fresh baked goods and home-cooked meals. There is nothing they wouldn't do for me."

Laura smiled widely as she mused, "Cole is a different story. He never says much about my cooking, but I can tell it in his eyes. For a man who rides desolate trails all of his life, whenever he slices into a thick beef steak, his eyes light up and you can see the pure pleasure he takes in savoring a meal home-cooked. I understand that a lot of womenfolk along his trails just wait for the opportunity to cook him a meal."

Most women in the West had little or no say when it came to men things, but when at home, there was a lot to say when supper time came. A wife who felt appreciated and loved would undoubtedly cook with love; those that felt less than appreciated, cooked likewise.

Anyway, on this morning, thunder reverberated through the air, lightning flashed, and torrents of rain flooded the trails. It was a storm such as most travelers had never seen the likes. The men ate like there was no tomorrow and called for cup after cup of that good coffee. All eyes were on the weather.

Laura looked over the waiting passengers and, to pass the time, tried to guess what they were like. The other woman she figured for a *society* type. She didn't help out with any chores, but expected to be waited upon. Laura considered her a real priss.

The one girl that helped with breakfast came up to Laura and introduced herself as Estelle Sanders and they talked a bit. She mentioned that she was going southwest to Santa Fe to find a good man, but if it didn't happen, she would be satisfied to just have a job where she could be herself and stake out a bit of savings for the future. Laura admired her ambition, and they got along fine.

The society woman looked over at Laura who was wearing boots and jeans and sort of snubbed her nose in the air. Laura wondered then just how she won her husband. After watching her husband for a while, she figured him for a timid little man who needed the security of a mother figure. He was a salesman of sorts, but had lots of money—he dealt in WHISKEY.

After observing two other coach passengers, Laura was glad that she was with Cole Stockton. These other men looked hard and willing. She shivered a bit when she looked into each man's eyes. She felt the slither of a snake. She watched them a bit longer and they periodically glanced over at the safe where the mail and express pouches were kept. She wondered about them and mentioned their obvious interest to Cole.

Cole responded, "Thanks Laura. I've already been told by a few others to watch out for these guys. Your observations confirm what I expect. You are still a Deputy U.S. Marshal and if you see anything out of the ordinary—take appropriate action."

Laura watched those two men mighty close from that point until the next morn when the storm finally cleared and they forked their ponies and rode on out.

Cole noticed that a couple of passengers breathed a lot easier after those two left.

Sammy and the station boys wrangled up the coach and hitched up the team. Sammy was real excited. This was his life—riding the high box and getting folks where they wanted to go. Jeb stood to one side, scrutinizing the passengers.

One of the men passengers, a real dandy, turned to Laura suddenly. He wore a fancy two-gun shoulder holster rig. He sort of held his coat open so she could see the pistol butts on either side of his chest. He was rather well built.

"Excuse me, Miss. I watched you in the station house and you are some kind of woman. You wear that gun belt like you know how to use it. I also am a man of the gun. My name is Cliff Houser. Perhaps you have heard of me. I am the fastest gun west of the Mississippi. I sure would like you to be MY lady friend."

Laura turned to face the man.

"Mr. Houser, I don't think that you could outdraw me, let alone my special friend. However, I'll give you one chance to prove yourself. Do you see that man standing out on the steps? The tall man wearing the dark blue shirt with yellow bandana? I'll tell you what, you walk right up to COLE STOCKTON and you tell him that you WANT his Lady Friend for your own. If he doesn't shoot you right then—I will."

Cliff Houser's face turned white as a sheet. Laura looked at him and grinned.

"Mister Houser, were I you, I'd turn your Eastern thoughts of gunplay back to wherever it was that you came from. I just looked into your eyes and you don't have one chance in Hell of matching a real Western gunfighter face to face. You'll be killed the first time you touch a gun. However, if you still want to make a home in the West, just be yourself."

Houser looked straight into her eyes with a most pitiful look on his face. "Ma'am, you read me right. I was a store keeper back in Massachusetts. I've read all the dime novels and bought me this pair of revolvers. I've practiced and practiced. I know that I am fast and can hit targets as small as bottle necks from whiskey bottles. I thought that I was real good and was ready to prove it. Is that really Cole Stockton? I mean, Cole Stockton, the gunfighter?"

"Yes, Cliff. That IS Cole Stockton, and I am his special friend. Should you want to prove it, just challenge him. I'll put flowers on your grave before we leave this station."

Cliff Houser swallowed hard. He exhaled a long sigh of relief and shook his head.

"I've bullied my way this far west just by sheer nerve. I am hi-strung and wanting of a good night's sleep. But, there were men—Western men that backed away from me when I confronted them."

"Well, Cliff, those men were probably ranchers, farmers, store keepers, plain cowhands, and such—men who are afraid of the gun. Mark my words. If you don't turn back now, there will come a day, very close to hand, that you will face a man who is hard bitten, vicious, and will stop at nothing to kill you. He will not talk nor reason with you. He will just shoot you dead."

Laura hesitated for only a moment before continuing, "Cole has a saying. Let a man carry a gun that knows how and when to use it. Let it be without remorse, for the first bullet must quell the situation. Secondly, prepare yourself to take lead. Any man that goes into a gunfight and thinks that he will NOT be shot is doomed to die."

"Mr. Houser, I have seen Cole Stockton lying on a table, naked and bleeding from gunshot wounds, and still his fingers were cocking and firing his revolver. A true gunfighter is hard to kill. Please don't make the mistake of thinking that you are fast, just because you can shoot some targets. I have seen Cole draw and shoot down whiskey bottle necks with six out of six bullets. More so, I have seen him draw and shoot several men, bragging just as you, straight in the chest two to three times and not even think about it. Is this what you want to be? A man who lives day by day, always wondering if the next man you meet will kill you. If that is what you want, then start with the best. Start with Cole Stockton and be laid to grave right now."

"No!" replied Houser, his voice shaky "I can't do it! I have never faced a man. Always I've relied on my skill at shooting targets. I only came west to try and prove my skills. I prayed that I would never meet face to face, such men as Bill Hickock, Wyatt Earp, Ben Thompson, William Bonney, or Cole Stockton. I just wanted to be somebody important."

Laura smiled at the man, "Cliff, out here in the West, store keepers are VERY important. They are the mainstay of a man's credibility. Out here, a man gives his word to pay by a handshake. The bargain is made and all parties abide. The man that knows the ways and wherefores of storekeeping, as well as accounting for the money, has got a real future in the West. Those that live by the gun generally die by the gun, unless you are extremely good, and let's face it, Cliff. I can outdraw you any day of the week."

"Oh, yeah? DRAW!" Cliff Houser reached for his left shoulder gun and stopped in mid-stride. Laura flashed her Colt .38 Lightning to his face, and once again, he turned white as a brand new sheet.

"Don't make me shoot you, Cliff. Haven't you heard a word I've said to you?"

He backed down and just about that time, Cole strode on over. He took one look at the Colt in Laura's hand and that knowing grin spread wide over his face.

"Mr. Houser, were it me that drew against you, we would be burying you this afternoon."

Cliff Houser got the very strong warning.

* *

A few hours later, the coach was ready, and the trail was dry enough. Sammy called for the passengers to board. Cole and Laura finished saddling Warrior and Mickey and settled packs on their led horse.

Cliff Houser, both women, and the whiskey salesman boarded the coach. Sammy grinned at Jeb who nodded his readiness and then, Sammy let out with a loud, "Hee Yaw! Get up now, come on youse crow baits. Let's stretch out into that harness!"

The coach lurched hard forward and the rear wheels kind of spun a bit, throwing mud and small stones at least five yards back. The station agent and several hostlers ducked quickly to the station porch to avoid being showered with the black ooze. The travelers were on their way.

Cole and Laura put boot to stirrup and swung easily up into the saddle. They rode slow and easy, following the deep trail left by the iron rims of the coach wheels.

* *

Jake Parnell and Duke Fenster waited silently five miles down the road between a large boulder and a thick stand of pines. Both men had scrutinized the overnight station safe and knew that the two of them couldn't take action there. They planned their alternate move—to take the coach on a curve in the road. Their plan was simple. Just ride out and shoot down the guard and whoever else threw up arms against them. They would take the money pouches and disappear into the wilds.

"What if that Marshal is still trailing that coach?" One man asked the other.

"Well, what of it, Duke? It won't be the first time I kilt me a lawman. Iffen he gets in the way, or trails us, we will lay for him and make sure that he never lives to trail anyone again."

A minute later, Parnell spoke, "Get ready, Duke, I hear the coach coming."

Both men drew their rifles and waited with narrowing eyes and set jaws.

* *

Sammy Colter eased back on the reins to slow the coach around the curve in the road. Suddenly, two rifle shots cracked the stillness. Jeb Wilson slammed back against the high-box seat back and then toppled from the coach to lie still at the side of the road. Sammy jerked hard back on the reins and slammed on the foot brake. Inside the coach, the women screamed with fright.

The two hard-bitten outlaws rode quickly out of their hiding place and commanded "Driver! Throw down those money pouches. Hurry now, or I'll blow you off of that seat."

Inside the coach, Cliff Houser swallowed hard, drew his right hand revolver and dived out of the coach door. He hit the ground, rolled, and came up leveling his gun at Duke Fenster. He fired.

Fenster jerked with the impact of a .44 slug through the shoulder. He recoiled, and then shot Cliff Houser straight in the chest. He sneered and then shot Cliff two more times. Houser died with the second bullet.

Sammy Colter calmly as possible reached down into the box storage and threw three express pouches to the ground. He looked hard at the two vicious men and burned their faces into his mind.

Jake Parnell dismounted just long enough to gather up the express pouches, hook one over Duke's saddle horn and two over his own saddle. He remounted and yelled at Duke, "Let's ride."

They galloped up through the boulders and pines and were out of sight within moments.

Sammy climbed down off the high-box and dashed to Jeb. He knew that the other young man, Cliff Houser, was already dead. The two women and other man inside the coach were still in a state of shock and just sat there—speechless and shaking.

"Jeb, you sorry excuse for a friend. You'd better not be dead. I'd never forgive you," Sammy pleaded.

Sammy turned Jeb over and examined the two gunshot wounds. One bullet had entered Jeb's right shoulder and the other had burned through his left side. Jeb was alive. Neither wound was life threatening.

"Damn it! Don't move me anymore, Sammy." Jeb ordered, choked with pain.

"Why not? You ain't gonna die."

"Not from the bullets, you fool. Can't you see that I broke my leg when I fell off the coach? Get something to splint it."

Just at that time, the younger woman from the coach, Estelle Sanders, regained her senses and stepped out to where Jeb and Sammy were. She looked at both of them for only an instant, then said, "Driver, find something to splint that leg, I'll get some cloth strips to wrap it."

Sammy was going to ask about the cloth strips when Estelle suddenly lifted her skirts and ripped off a petticoat. She began tearing it into long strips of cloth.

Jeb looked up at Sammy.

"Well, Sammy. Don't just stand there gawking. Go get the damn splints."

CHAPTER FIFTEEN

"Chasing the Outlaws"

Cole and Laura were taking their time riding back into the Lower Colorado, and enjoying the scenery. They were about three miles behind the coach when Cole suddenly pulled up and listened.

"Laura, that sounds like gunfire up ahead."

A moment later, several quick sharp cracks followed, one after the other.

"That's revolver fire! I think that the coach is in trouble. Let's ride!" Cole's words demanded.

Cole handed the lead rope to the pack horse to Laura and put spur to Warrior's flanks. Laura heeled Mickey into a fast trot and spoke to the pack animal, "Come, little one! Keep up with us."

Twenty some minutes later, Cole rounded the bend to find the coach stopped. Sammy and Estelle were helping a wounded Jeb into the coach.

When Laura caught up to the coach, Cole was kneeling over a man on the ground. She glanced at the man covered with a blanket, and felt a quick stab of sorrow. Seeing the fancy boots of the covered body, she knew that Cliff Houser was the man on the ground and that he was dead.

Sammy was relating the scene to Cole as Laura dismounted and looked down at Cliff. She couldn't help the slight mist as it formed in her eyes. She mused, "He was young, and he was foolish, but he was following his dream."

She wondered then if the outcome of this holdup would have been different if Cole and she had been riding alongside the coach.

Laura turned toward Sammy who was speaking, "Yah, Cole. Them guys gave us no warning. They just up and shot Jeb off of the high-box. When they came ariding out of the trees over there, the kid jumped out of the coach, hit the ground, and shot one of them. He must've have fired too fast, cause he only wounded the SOB. That's when the man he shot turned on him and shot him two or three times. The last one wasn't necessary. He meant to kill him. They rode around that boulder and up into the trees. They was a whipping steam to them hosses, too. I think that they are headed for the wilds. Anyway, Cole, the kid tried to stop it. He had nerve."

"Yes, Sammy, he had nerve, but he didn't have the sense to keep shooting. I'm going after them. These guys are vicious killers and I'll see them to Hell or hang for it."

Cole walked to Warrior, looked at Laura, and said, "Laura. I'm going after those guys. You can ride along with the coach and see them to the next stop. I'll catch up after I run these killers down."

"Not on your life, Cole Stockton! I'm riding with you. Don't you try to dissuade me, my mind is made up. One of those guys killed that young man, and I am determined that there will be justice. Besides, I am still YOUR Deputy."

"Oh, Hell! All right, Deputy, let's ride."

* *

Cole led out and they rode up between the boulders and the pine stand where the two men had waited for the coach. He pulled up, dismounted, and walked slowly all around the area looking for any possible evidence.

"Cole, those guys are getting away. We need to follow them," offered up Laura.

"Laura, those men were here for at least a couple of hours. I'm looking for clues as to their habits, if any, and anything else I can find out about them."

Laura thought to herself then, "I would never have thought about that. I just wanted to ride hard and catch up with them. Cole is right, though, I could see it. He is studying those men. He is learning all about them. He is learning the way that they think, act, and to some extent, their makeup. That they were both vicious killers was already known. To what extent that they would fight was still to be determined."

"At least one of them likes his tobacco," pointed out Cole. "Look here, Laura. He smokes his homemades right down to the last. That also tells me that they might be short on money. By the droppings of their horses, they were here for about five hours. They ate nothing, so they should be looking for a meal shortly. That they used rifles first off tells me that they like to lie at long range and shoot. They want an advantage. They probably are good with handguns, but are most likely short of ammunition. The one that shot that kid used a .44 revolver—common, but effective."

After a few moments, Cole continued, "The kid put some lead into one of them. They will be looking for a doctor somewhere. By the way that Sammy described the shooting, the wounded man will be feeling poorly about now. If the lead passed on through him, he will still need attention for sterilization. If it didn't, he needs that bullet removed. I figure that the nearest doctor is close to Fort Fetterman or possibly some homesteader. My bet is that they are making for Cheyenne: after that, they are in MY COUNTRY, the Lower Colorado Wilds. Well, Laura. They have only a short head start. We'll catch up to them within a few hours from now, that is, unless they lie low to watch their back trail. Look for anything out of the ordinary."

Cole climbed back into the saddle. Laura marveled at the information he gleaned from just looking around the area.

She thought, "I would have never thought to look for those things."

Cole found the trail and pointed out to Laura that one horse had a large ragged chip missing from its left hind shoe. He also watched the spacing of the tracks and determined that they were riding fast and hard.

"They've got to slow down pretty soon or kill their horses. They should rest for a while and then, we'll gain on them. We'll continue at a steady pace, resting for fifteen minutes every hour. It may not seem like too much, but we'll gain valuable ground on them. I figure to catch up to them by tomorrow morning, and then all Hell will break loose.

Cole knew his business. He was pointing out things that any fast moving posse might overlook and those factors might prove the difference between finding these men or missing them completely. He also knew the limit of Warrior and Mickey, and wanted them rested as much as possible. They might need them for a hard chase.

Laura wondered why Cole sort of zig-zagged while he rode.

"Are you down with the heat or something Cole? You seem to be zig-zagging all over the trail."

"There is a method to this madness, Laura. Sometimes a rider will drop off his horse and angle off for a bit. They will especially do this when an ambush site comes up. The Apache use this trick quite often to get suddenly behind their quarry. Watch for the depth of the tracks. If a horse suddenly loses depth, it's a sure sign that the rider has gotten off somewhere and is behind you."

The more Laura rode along with Cole on a hunt, the more she marveled at his savvy of the trails.

"Other things to watch for are a sudden flush of birds, NO sound of nature, and your horse's ears suddenly pricked up. Of course, there is the old fashioned way of the *hairs* on the back of your neck standing straight up. Personally, I'd heed all of these signs. Like right now, looking at those tracks, I'd say that one man is leaning down over his horse's neck and is being led."

"How can you tell, Cole?"

"Look at how close those tracks are to the other. Yes, one is being led. They are slowing down some. Look at the spacing of the tracks."

Cole suddenly pulled up short and dashed to the ground. He bent over intently and examined the smashed grass.

"The wounded man is bleeding. Here is a drop of blood—there's another. Well now, they have a situation. They either have to stop soon, or one will bleed to death."

* *

Duke Fenster felt the throbbing pain now through his entire body. A shiver of hot fever seared through his flesh and he felt the sweat pop out on his brow. That *kid* had put lead into him and now it was bothering him. He closed his eyes for a long moment. When he opened them, he stared blurry-eyed ahead at his partner, Jake. Jake was riding steadily upward through the trees.

Duke called out as loud as he could, "Jake! Help me! I can't shake this chill."

Jake halted his dun for a moment until the swaying figure rode up beside him. He stared deep into Duke's eyes and saw the pain and fever. He calmly drew his Colt Revolver and shot Duke right in the face. Duke's limp body jolted out of the saddle and sprawled flat on the ground.

Jake dismounted only long enough to search and take any money that Duke had in his pockets. He also unbuckled Duke's gunbelt and laid it across his saddle.

He thought, "Might need the extra ammunition."

Jake took the express pouches from his saddle and hung them around Duke's saddle. He thought,

"Only twenty miles to go, and I'll cut open these bags. Maybe I can sell Duke's horse somewhere. I'll head for the wilds of Colorado. There are places there that the Indians don't even know about. I'll lay low for a month or so and then travel to Old Mexico. A man can live like a king down there with this money."

Jake turned his horse and trailing Duke's sorrel, made for the wild Colorado.

* *

The outlaw's trail headed toward the foothills to the Rockies close to Cheyenne. From that point, it was only about a hundred miles into the wilds of Colorado. The landscape was upward rolling hills. Some areas were covered in thick pine and spruce, and others with extremely thick brush. There were also a lot open high-grassed areas.

Cole and Laura traveled several miles further and the land was sloping upward when the horses pricked up their ears. The pack horse shied and Laura had to pull hard on the lead rope to bring him along.

That's when they saw the body lying in the brush. Cole dismounted and walked up to the dead man. After a long moment, he turned to Laura, "It looks like our wounded killer was holding his partner back and slowing him down. He's been shot at close range. We'll camp here for the night. Set up a small fire a bit away from here, and get some coffee going. I'll do the digging and burying."

Cole got the small shovel from the pack animal again and stripped off his shirt. Burying the dead just came with the job.

Laura picketed the horses about twenty yards away and got a fire going. She unpacked the skillet and got some bacon frying. She dumped two cans of beans in the skillet with that crisp bacon and quickly stirred dough for about a half dozen dropped flour biscuits for the Dutch oven. It wasn't much, but it was a sight better than cold jerky and hard biscuits.

The coffee was just right when Cole threw the last shovel full of dirt on the mound and tamped it down. He found a large rock and scratched the date on it, with a short inscription that read:

April 1879

Outlaw / Killer

Murdered by partner

Cole placed the rock at the head of the grave, then said a few words for the departed soul. In his eyes, even a vicious outlaw has to answer for his crimes in the court of the Almighty.

Regardless of the circumstances, riding the trails like this, people got mighty hungry. The beans, bacon, biscuits and coffee was like a feast to them. Afterward, Cole rolled a smoke and the two of them lay back against their saddles and relaxed. Winchester Rifles were close to hand as this was still the land of the Cheyenne and Arapaho.

The next day started early. The sun was just peeking over the land from the east when Cole and Laura swung up into their saddles. They could just make out the tracks of the other outlaw and the led horse.

By noon it was obvious that the man was headed toward the

Colorado Territory and the wilds. Cole grinned and sort of chuckled to himself.

"Well, now. He is headed right into MY country." Laura nodded.

Twenty miles further they rode up to a small homestead. They approached slowly. Cole surveyed the small corral, taking note of the stock. There was a sorrel that appeared out of place. This was a working farm and that sorrel was definitely saddle stock.

Cole hailed the house as they drew up at the front door. A middle aged, rangy-looking man with heavy beard stepped out to the small porch. He looked his visitors us up and down suspiciously.

"Howdy!" Cole said. "We're following a friend. That sorrel looks mighty familiar. How did you come by it?"

The settler stroked his beard for a moment, scowling, before replying, "W-e-l-l, now. That's none of your business is it?"

Cole looked deep into the man's eyes, reached into his vest pocket and pinned on the Silver Star.

"I just made it my business. Now, how and when did you come by that sorrel?"

"Sorry, Marshal," The homesteader quickly changed his tune, "feller came through here early this morning. He was in need of some grub and other supplies. I traded supplies and twenty dollars cash money for that horse. He gave me a bill of sale."

"I don't question that. You can keep the horse. What did this man look like and which way did he ride? Tell me everything about the man that you can remember."

Cole and Laura dismounted and watered their horses while the homesteader related all he knew about the outlaw. An hour later they rode out toward Colorado Territory. Their quarry was only five hours ahead of them now. Once again, they were gaining ground on him.

* *

Jake Parnell felt smugly satisfied with himself. He had stopped briefly, cut open the express bags and found close to fifty thousand dollars in currency and gold coin. He smiled crookedly as he stuffed the bills and coins into the two sets of saddle bags. He took the three empty express bags and flung them into a rocky crevice. He had fifty thousand dollars and no one to share it with. He would live like a king down in Mexico.

He thought to himself, "Too bad about Duke getting shot by that kid. That was his bad luck. If he just hadn't been slowing us down. I'll drink to him next time I get to a saloon."

Jake remounted and looked toward the distant mountains. He now had supplies enough to last three or four days and by then he would be deep in the Wilds of the Colorado.

There were small towns in Colorado where he was unknown and could safely pick up more supplies. There were abandoned trapper cabins where he could lie low for weeks and no one would be the wiser.

Jake Parnell knew exactly where he was headed. He had traveled the Wilds before and knew of one cabin in particular that would meet his need. He spurred his dun into a fast trot. With luck, he would be there the next day.

Three hours later he was riding along the ridges in the Colorado Territory. Suddenly, the hairs on the back of his neck seemed to prick up. A nagging feeling began to pick at his brain. He felt uneasy.

Jake pulled up on a high point and watched the distance of his back trail. A slight movement. Then, he saw them. Two riders and a pack horse. The lead rider seemed to be studying the ground. A tracker!

Jake watched the riders closely. He realized that they were tracking him. He cursed.

"Dammit all to Hell! That must be that Marshal. He's been tracking me all the way from Montana. I'll fix him. I'll fix him real good."

Jake Parnell tied his horse to a tree, then slid his rifle out and climbed to an advantage point. He watched in grim silence as the two riders neared rifle range. He jacked a round into the chamber and lined his sights on the *tracker*. He took a deep breath, held it an instant, then squeezed the trigger.

The rifle bucked against his cheek and shoulder as .44-40 lead sailed toward his pursuers. He watched as the man toppled from his dark chestnut horse to lie unmoving on the ground. The second rider pulled up short, grabbed a Winchester and hit the ground. The horses trotted a distance away.

Jake levered another bullet in the chamber and fired again. Dirt pillowed up next to the second rider. He saw the puff of smoke from the rider's carbine. A split second later molten lead whistled past his left ear and whined into space. Jake fired again and again. He missed with both shots. The second rider was rolling in different directions and each time Jake's bullet struck the earth, the rider would fire at Jake's rifle smoke. One bullet struck the rock directly in front of Jake and spattered fragments into his face.

"Damn, that guy. He's good with that long gun. I got one of them anyway. That'll slow them down. I'm going to get the Hell out of here—and fast!"

Jake stood up slightly to turn toward his horse. Another bullet burned through his sleeve and he felt the sting. He winced, but still dashed to his horse, tore the reins from the tree, and practically leaped into the saddle, sinking spur to his animal.

Jake broke into a hard run along the slope and disappeared into the tree line. He rode hard and furious for close to an hour. He stopped then, and walked his mount. He rolled up his sleeve and examined his arm. The bullet had just grazed him. There was dried blood caked along the crease.

Jake opened his saddlebags, retrieved an old shirt and tore it into strips. He bandaged the slight wound, then remounted and rode steadily toward the Lower Colorado.

"To Hell with this! I've changed my mind. I'll stop in that little town just before the mountain passes into New Mexico for one day. Then, I'll ride straight for Mexico and safety."

CHAPTER SIXTEEN

"Laura's Dilemma"

Cole Stockton had been concentrating on the tracks before him when the sudden jolt of a rifle bullet slammed him off Warrior. The report of the rifle sounded a split second later.

Laura Sumner's eyes went wide as she watched Cole suddenly jerk off Warrior and lie deathly still on the hard ground. She reacted immediately.

Laura reached back and drew her own Winchester, dived out of Mickey's saddle, and hit the ground rolling to one side.

"Go Mickey! Go Warrior! Get out of here!"

Both horses turned and trotted away to stand almost a hundred yards back down the trail. The pack horse followed suit.

Laura's determined, but misty eyes searched the high ground and along the boulder strewn ridge. Suddenly a whiz and dirt furrowed up alongside Laura. She saw the puff of smoke and squeezed off a round directly at the puff.

Two more puffs followed in close succession. Laura immediately rolled to the left and fired, then rolled back to the right and fired again. She heard her second bullet as it smacked into rock and splattered up dust and fragments. Two more bullets smacked into the ground on either side of her. Laura saw a quick movement and fired again. Then, all was silent.

She looked over at Cole who lay sprawled on his back—unmoving. She saw the blood spreading along his right shoulder.

Laura cautiously crawled over to Cole Stockton and looked directly into his face. He was out cold. His breathing was shallow and she knew that he was in shock. She had to stop the bleeding.

Laura tore open Cole's shirt and examined him. The bullet was imbedded deep in his right shoulder and had to come out. Immediately, she tore Cole's shirt into strips and pieces. She bound the wound to temporarily stop the bleeding. She would have to get the horses and set up a camp.

Laura took a deep breath. That bullet had to come out and she knew that she was the one who had to do it. There was no one else to depend on.

She would have to take care of both of them.

"Can I do it? Am I a good enough doctor?" she questioned herself.

* *

Laura called to Mickey and Warrior. Both horses came at a fast trot and stopped just a foot from her. The pack horse seemed to balk.

"Probably senses Cole's blood," thought Laura. "Mickey, go bring that pack horse back here."

Mickey turned and trotted to the pack horse that immediately shied away. Mickey was trained to corner and herd wild horses, and he was relentless in his pursuit of the reluctant animal. After several long minutes, Mickey finally turned and herded the pack animal back to Laura.

Laura picketed the pack horse and dropped the packs off. She built a small fire and began to heat water in a small pan. She got out the knife and tested its edge. It would need to be a lot sharper. She took out a whetstone and began sliding the long blade back and forth over the stone.

Within ten minutes, the edge on the hunting knife was like a razor. She laid the knife in the red hot coals of the fire to sterilize it.

Laura also rummaged through the packs and found a half bottle of the amber-colored liquid fire—whiskey. She looked at the bottle in her hand, then looked at Cole Stockton.

"Oh, what the Hell! I need a steady hand."

She took a quick slug of the strong liquid. She closed her eyes as she felt the slow burn all the way down her throat. She exhaled.

"O.K., I guess that I'm ready."

Laura moved to the still unconscious Cole. She removed the binding and padding. The bleeding had stopped and dried blood stuck to the padding. She got her canteen and soaked the pad, then eased the padding away from the wound.

Laura swallowed hard, then took her finger and pushed it into the bullet hole. She needed to find out how deep the lead was. She found it about an inch and a half into the shoulder muscle.

Next, she took the bottle of whiskey and poured a good amount into the wound. It began to bleed somewhat again. She reached into the fire and taking the red hot, razor sharp hunting knife, held it for a minute, then slid it into Cole's shoulder along the edge of the bullet. She held it there with one hand while she took her other hand and probed her index finger down into the wound. She, as gently as possible, moved the knife slightly to dislodge the bullet. She felt it move.

Slowly, painfully, she probed her finger underneath the hard lead and then began the heart-wrenching task of slowly sliding it up and out of the hole, keeping the knife blade alongside of the lead.

Long minutes ticked by and sweat poured down Laura's face and down her body. The salty substance burned her, eyes but she blinked the sweat away and kept at the arduous task.

Finally the bullet slipped up and out of the hole. Blood flowed freely with the bullet. Laura took the chunk of lead with her blood soaked fingers and looked at it. She exhaled a great sigh of relief. The bullet was intact and had not spread nor broken.

Quickly, she took the hot water and cleaned the wound, then poured another measure of whiskey into it. She placed a clean pad over the hole and secured it into place with strips of cloth. She looked at Cole. In spite of her crude surgery, Cole was still unconscious. She knew that was a blessing. She hoped he hadn't felt a thing. He was sweating and starting to shiver, but he was alive. She fed him a spoonful of whiskey and made him swallow it by stroking his throat.

Laura gathered up blankets and covered the wounded Marshal. She sat beside him and soaked his face with cool water in an effort to drop the fever.

Several hours passed before Cole began to breathe easy and she noticed that his hands were relaxed. She pulled off his boots and set them aside. She felt his forehead and found it somewhat cool. He was out of shock and appeared to be sleeping.

Then and only then did Laura sit back and breathe normally herself. She looked at the whiskey bottle and took another swallow. Once again the amber liquid burned all the way down to her stomach.

She stood up and unsaddled the horses, letting them continue to graze. She suddenly realized that she was hungry.

As Laura prepared a meager meal of bacon, a small baked potato, canned beans, a couple of biscuits, and coffee, she also shaved some jerky into a small pot of boiling hot water. She made a broth for Cole. She would feed it to him when he came around.

Finally, she sat back with her plate of food. It was only then that she began to think.

"What if," she thought, "what if I had done as Cole had wanted and stayed with the stage-coach. God, that killer could have shot him and then come down here and finished him off. It would be days before anyone found him."

She realized that it was their *bond* of love and understanding that tempered fate and kept them together. It was her bond of love for him that enabled her to perform the crude surgery that removed the bullet from his shoulder. It was the bond of love that now placed his welfare in her hands.

Laura thought of these things. She also thought of the murderous outlaw who had lain in wait and attempted to kill them both. She became angry. She wanted to face that man and shoot him down just as uncaring and unremorseful as he had shot Cole. She wanted to look deep into his eyes and see the pain of hot lead as it tore into his body. She wanted to kill that man.

She made up her mind. They were within a day's ride of her ranch.

She would take Cole directly to Doctor Simmons, then get some of her wranglers and track that man down. She would insure a hard justice.

* *

It was near to midnight and the campfire burned low. Laura Sumner was leaning back against her saddle and blankets dozing. Her Colt Lightning Revolver sat close to her hand.

She sensed, rather than heard the first low moan. Her eyes popped open and she listened intently. Another moan and then Cole Stockton moved. He tried to sit up, groaned and fell back exhausted. Laura heard him mumble.

"Damn, I'm sore. I feel like I've been kicked in the chest and shoulder by a mule."

Laura was immediately beside him, looking down into his pained face. Her eyes misted a bit and a caring smile of relief spread across her face.

"Just lie still, Cole. You've been shot. We were ambushed by that man we're tracking. There was no way you could have seen it coming. He was high up and not visible. I got the bullet out and you'll be all right. You just need rest. I've got some broth for you."

"You   got   the   bullet?"

"Yes. I got the bullet. It took me a swig of your whiskey and a long time, but I got it out."

"Well I'll be," he stammered. "You are getting right handy at being around just when I need you. I guess this means that I should keep you around for a <u>long, long time</u>."

She looked at him tenderly as a pained grin spread suddenly across his face. She could feel the bonds of love radiating from his eyes and she bent forward kiss him tenderly.

He tried to move his arm around her.

"Ouch! That throbs something fierce. My right hand feels kind of numb. Guess I won't be shooting any guns with it for a while."

"You just lie still, Cole Stockton. I'll take care of any shooting for both of us until you are well again."

* *

The next morning, Laura rigged a travois from some blankets and some poles she cut from tender saplings. She slung the poles into the stirrups on Warrior's saddle, tied them securely with rawhide strips, then helped Cole climb into the makeshift stretcher. The going would be slow and bumpy, but easier on Cole than riding a horse at this point.

"If you need to stop, you yell out, Cole. I'll go as easy as I can."

Laura led out riding Mickey and leading both Warrior and the pack horse. With luck, they could reach the town and the doctor by sundown."

* *

Jake Parnell dismounted wearily in front of the large two-story hotel. He had ridden all night long and he was tired and hungry. He could get a room in this little town and the next day ride down the mountain passes into New Mexico and toward final freedom.

He immediately removed the two heavy saddle bags from his horse and pulled his Winchester from the boot. He entered the hotel and registered at the desk.

"I'll be here until tomorrow. Have my horse, the dun just outside, taken to the livery. I'll pick him up around dawn tomorrow."

He also asked about the best saloon and the best eating house in town. He then went to his room to wash up and get some much needed rest.

The hotel clerk hailed the young boy that performed odd jobs.

"Take that dun horse over to the livery and tell Mr. Jackson that the owner is registered at the hotel and that he will call for his animal tomorrow morning."

The boy ran out the door and led the horse to the livery.

The clerk turned back to his work when he heard footsteps moving across the floor toward him. He looked up from his task and said, "Good Morning, Sheriff Kincaid. It looks like a hot one again today."

Sheriff J. C. Kincaid nodded his agreement.

"Say, Warren. I got an interesting telegram yesterday. Been meaning to come over here and inquire. I want you to let me know if any strangers, about two of them—rough looking men, one may be favoring an arm, happen to stop in here for lodging. They may be wanted men. I will want to check them out."

"Yes, Sir, Sheriff. No, I haven't seen TWO men. There is ONE man, though. He arrived just a bit ago carrying two heavy saddle bags. He looked mighty tired, like he had traveled a long ways. He said that he was staying until tomorrow morning. I'd say that he is sound asleep by now."

"O.K., Warren. I'd like to speak to this man a bit later. Let me know when he comes down."

* *

The going was slow indeed and after two hours, Cole called for a halt. Laura pulled up, dismounted, and moved around to Cole. He was sweating and complained about his shoulder feeling awful sore.

Laura removed the blanket covering him. His fresh shirt and the bandage were soaked with fluid and blood. The wound appeared somewhat swollen.

"Cole. I've got to open that wound again and let it drain some. It looks like it is festering some. I wish that I had something besides that whiskey to put on it."

No sooner had she spoken, when the sound of hoof beats caught Laura's attention and she looked up. A lone rider was coming toward them at a fairly fast clip. She watched him for a long minute. Then smiled and waved.

Spotted Hawk, the Indian scout from Fort Lyon, brought his pony to a dust-swirling halt beside the small entourage. He leaped to the ground and made known his gladness at seeing Laura once again. He looked at Cole Stockton and shook his head side to side.

He bent over the wounded Marshal and examined, then probed and squeezed the wound. Cole winced with the touch.

"Mighty Warrior need <u>big medicine</u>. Many times I have seen this wound. I fix for you."

Spotted Hawk went to his saddle pack and rummaged. Within a few minutes, he brought out a small mixing bowl, a crude grinding tool, and some foul-smelling powder. He took the whiskey bottle from Laura, looked at it and took a long swallow. He grinned from ear to ear. Then he poured a measure of the amber liquid into the small bowl. He put a pinch or two of the foul-smelling powder into it, then took a handful of mud that he had mixed and mashed it all together in the bowl. He smelled the concoction and nodded his satisfaction.

The scout turned to Cole and spread the smelly substance all over the wound. He took the fresh bandage that Laura offered and secured it over the poultice. He grinned.

"Big medicine! Mar-shall Stockton be strong like grizzly bear in two suns."

Cole looked up at the both of them and replied, "I don't know what is worse; bumping around on this travois, the throbbing in my shoulder, or the smell of this here big medicine."

The three of them laughed loudly.

Spotted Hawk rode with them for several miles and then had to turn off as he was carrying important dispatches. He waved his respect as he veered off and disappeared into the tree line.

Laura and Cole continued toward home. They looked to arrive sometime after midnight.

* *

Cole and Laura arrived in their small town sometime after midnight. She took Cole immediately to Doctor Simmons' office and rousted him out before helping Cole inside the front door.

Doc Simmons hurriedly pulled his trousers over his night shirt and splashed water on his face. He turned to Cole and stripping off his shirt and bandage, began to examine the poultice.

He carefully pulled back on the muddy, smelly mixture until he could see the wound itself. After a long minute, he remarked,

"Well, Cole, there is nothing I can do for you. The wound is clean and whatever is in this poultice has absorbed any poison from your system. Who took the bullet out?"

Laura had to confess that it was she.

"You did a good job, Laura. He won't be using that right shoulder for a couple of weeks, but that's about normal for this type of gunshot wound."

They thanked Doctor Simmons and decided to get rooms in the hotel for the night, it being late and all. A good night's rest in a bed would do wonders for the both of them.

Laura dropped Cole at the hotel steps and then took the horses over to the livery. She advised Mr. Jackson that she and Cole would pick up their mounts in the morning.

Laura went back to the hotel to find that Cole had already gotten them two rooms. Their rooms, as usual, were across the hall from each other.

Half an hour later, Laura lay back on the pillow and drifted off to sleep. She dreamed of a mean and ugly-looking man of darkened soul. He was standing on a wooden porch with two bags of gold in one hand and a smoking Colt Revolver in the other. His eyes were fierce and the aura of death surrounded him.

* *

Laura was up with the first rays of the sun and stumbled down the hall to the washroom. A quick dip in a tub of nicely heated water with scented soap was refreshing.

After dressing, she went to Cole's room and lightly rapped on the door. It opened immediately. He stood there stripped to the waist and face all lathered up with shaving soap. His razor lay next to the wash basin and he had that usual grin on his face.

"Glad that you're up," he said. "I could use some assistance. I don't normally shave with my left hand and I'd sure hate to add a cut throat to my other misery."

She laughed. Cole was in good spirits. That meant that he was feeling much better.

She stepped into his room and closed the door. Cole sat down in the straight backed wooden chair and Laura shaved him. Once he was slick faced, she suddenly took it upon herself to bend over to give him a kiss, avoiding touching his wounded shoulder. They gingerly embraced and she could feel the warmth of his soul.

A few minutes later, Cole tried to strap his gunbelt on, without much luck.

"Here, Cole. Let me help you. How do you want it?"

"Oh, let's slide it around to my left side, butt forward. I can draw and fire with my left hand in a reverse draw. I'm not as fast that way, but it will have to do until I can use my right hand again."

The two of them went down through the hotel lobby and once on the boardwalk, Laura told Cole that she would walk down to the livery and check on their horses. He agreed and said that he wanted to talk to J.C. Kincaid for a few minutes. Cole walked toward the jail and Laura toward the livery.

Laura didn't know what made her look at the tracks in front of the open livery door, but suddenly, she saw hoof prints with a large ragged chip missing from the left rear shoe. They were the same tracks that Cole and she had been following.

The killer's horse was in the livery somewhere! She turned to Mr. Jackson, the livery hostler, and asked him what horses had been stabled within the past day.

Lee Jackson pointed out five horses and she went to each and examined the left rear shoe. The last horse, a dun, proved to be the horse in question.

"Who belongs to this animal?" she inquired.

"Some feller rode into town around late yesterday afternoon. He got a room at the hotel and had the errand boy bring his animal here. He said that he would claim it sometime this morning."

Laura thanked Jackson for the information and started toward the jail. She would get Cole and J.C. They would know what to do about the fugitive.

Laura was ten yards from the livery when the stagecoach rumbled into town and stopped at the express office, right across from the hotel. Sammy Colter climbed down from the high box and opened the door for the passengers. He turned around just as a stocky, bearded man stepped out of the hotel carrying two saddle bags and a Winchester.

Further down the street, Cole Stockton and J.C. Kincaid stepped out of the jail and started towards the hotel.

Sammy turned and looked straight into the eyes of Jake Parnell. He suddenly blurted it out, "You! You're one of them murderous coach robbers."

The stocky man suddenly dropped the Winchester and went for his revolver in the same motion. Sammy Colter reached for his revolver and dived under the coach.

J.C. Kincaid was drawing his revolver and Cole's hand flashed to his holster. Laura reached for her Colt Lightning at the same instant.

The killer fired at Sammy first, and then all hell broke loose. J.C. Kincaid's first bullet smacked into a hitching post right beside Parnell. The man turned and leveled his Colt at the sheriff and Cole.

Cole's revolver slid out of his holster and he hit the ground rolling to the right. He winced loudly as he hit on his right shoulder. J.C. dived behind a water trough. The killer's next bullet splintered through the trough, and J.C. got soaked with water.

Laura's Colt was in her hand. She squeezed off, and watched as dust pillowed up on the killer's vest. He turned as he staggered a bit and fired one directly at Laura. She felt the rush of hot air as the molten lead sailed through her jean jacket and smacked into the livery behind her. She fired at him again, but missed.

Somewhere in the middle of all this, Sammy Colter got off a couple of rounds from under the coach. He didn't hit anything, but it kept the killer on his toes, turning this way and that in feeble attempts to shoot at all four of them.

Cole fired now and the man grunted with the impact of .44 caliber lead as it hit him deep in the chest. He staggered back dropping the saddle bags but still stayed on his feet. He sneered and leveled his Colt once again at Cole.

Cole rolled to the left and fired again. This bullet only sailed the man's hat high into the air. Cole swore and then suddenly stood up.

He held that Colt in his left hand cocking it and firing bullet after bullet as he steadily walked toward the killer.

Laura vividly remembered the vicious ambush and got raging mad. She also walked toward the killer, firing as she walked. J.C. Kincaid stood up and did likewise. The air was filled with hot molten lead looking for victims.

The killer was caught in a three-pronged crossfire, but he tried to the last. Cole had stopped firing and was shoving fresh cartridges into the cylinder of his Colt when Laura lined up on the man.

She squeezed off and as the hot lead tore through his throat, he slammed back against the hotel wall and slid slowly to the ground. A trail of blood marked his path of descent.

She walked up to him and looked down upon the face of the killer. His unseeing eyes staring right at her, his mouth dropped open and his bleeding shot to pieces body leaning in a sitting position against the wall. His twitching hand held the now empty but still smoking Colt Revolver.

Laura said quietly, "I finally got you, you SOB."

Cole was suddenly beside her. He looked down on the killer for a long moment. Then he stepped in front of Laura. He gently took the revolver from her hand and slid it into her holster.

They looked deep into each other's eyes and felt the relief that they were both still alive. She put her arms tightly around him and leaned her head against his chest. There is no greater bond than the smoldering love between a man and HIS Lady.

CHAPTER SEVENTEEN

"Lonely is the Wind"

I never did completely understand women, and I guess that it was one of those things that just has to happen in some folks lives.

I'd risen with the dawn that day and quickly dressed, not paying much attention to anything.

I walked out to the kitchen and found Laura sitting at the table drinking a cup of coffee. She looked a bit distant and ragged around the eyes, like she had not slept all night.

I took a cup from the cupboard, walked over to the wood stove, and began filling it with fresh, rich, dark coffee. I sensed that her eyes were glued on me for some reason, and I turned to look at her.

"I've been thinking", she said.

"About what"?

"About a lot of things, Cole. One of which is the fact that you just took it upon yourself to move your things back into my house and set up housekeeping. A lot like you own me or something."

"Laura, I've never thought that, and you know it."

"Do I? It seems that everyone around here is taken with the idea that I'm <u>your woman</u>. Well, I am my own woman, and no one else's. As a matter of fact, I want you to move out of my house and back into the bunkhouse. Better yet, move into town. That way, you don't have to come and go, come and go, and come and go. You can be as close to your situations as possible.

"Now, just what has gotten into you, Laura? Is it something that I've said? Is it something that I've done to hurt your feelings? Please tell me what it is and I will apologize."

"Just go and move into town. I don't want to see you for a long time. I have to think things out in my mind."

"O.K., I will, and don't think I will be back anytime soon."

"Go! And the sooner the better."

"I will," I said, and set my cup down. I stomped out of the house.

I went to the barn and saddled up Warrior, then led him back to the house. I took the first step up onto the porch, when all of a sudden, the door flew open and all of my meager belongings came flying out. The door slammed shut behind them.

I stood there, stunned, and scratching my head. Just what the Devil had gotten into her?

Well, I gathered up my things as best that I could and stuffed them into a gunnysack that she had thrown out with them. That is, all except for the fine new suit that she had given me this past Christmas. I pondered about it, and decided that I didn't need a suit that fancy in my line of work, so I just folded it and left it sitting there on the porch.

I mounted Warrior and with a final look at the immaculately painted white frame ranch house and colorful flowerbeds, I turned and rode toward town. I never looked back, even though I had the distinct feeling that someone was watching me.

The hour-long ride to town was an eternity for me. I went back and forth over the events of the past few months in my mind, and for the life of me, I still couldn't figure out why she all of a sudden didn't want me around anymore.

Well, being a man of honor, at least I thought so, I decided to let things lie as they were and get on with my life.

I'd said it before. I didn't want a woman having to fret that when I rode out, that I wouldn't come back to her. That thought seemed to help a little. Still, I felt definite pangs of hurt and rejection, the first in a long time. That old sense of loneliness began to set in.

It was about ten in the morning, I reckon, when I finally entered the town and rode slowly up to the jailhouse. My Deputy, Toby Bodine, was still up in Creede, and the duly elected town Sheriff, J.C. Kincaid, sat idly whittling a stick out front of the jail. He looked kind of surprised when I pulled up laden down with all of my possessions in tow, but he kept his tongue. I guess that I really didn't look like friendly conversation. He just sucked on that long piece of grass and nodded hello to me. I gave him a half-hearted wave and hauled the gunnysack into the building.

After storing most of my life in various cabinets and drawers, I decided to have a cool beer and think things out. I opted for the *Lady Luck* Saloon. God knows that I could use all the luck I could get about now.

I tramped up the boardwalk and paused for a moment or two in front of the bat wing doors. I sighed heavily, then strode on in, right up to the bar. Louise Montrose, part owner and main attraction, looked at me with widened and questioning eyes. Funny, I had never really noticed her eyes before. They were big and brown and sort of dreamy looking.

"Marshal Stockton, is there something wrong? You never come in here except when there's big trouble."

"No, Louise, there's nothing wrong. I just decided to have a cool beer. Is that O.K.? You do have beer, don't you?"

"Ah, why yes, Marshal. We do have beer. After all, this is a saloon."

"Well, pour me a mug."

She did as I requested and I took it to a lone table in the back of the room. There I sat, my back to the wall, leaning back in the chair. My thoughts were miles away. I didn't even notice Louise walk up to me with a pot of coffee and two cups.

"Marshal," she said, "you don't appear to be the drinking type, and I sense that there is something worrying you. Could it be *woman* troubles? I think coffee is better than beer for clear thinking. Can I join you?"

I motioned her to take a seat.

"I'd rather have another beer," I said.

"You're the boss." She turned to the bartender, "Bring Marshal Stockton another beer—on the house."

That second beer was better than the first. Louise just sat there with me. She didn't say anything, but she smiled. That as more sunshine than I'd had all day long. Finally, I just looked at her and said, "I think

I'll ride up towards Creede for a few days. Thank you Louise, for your hospitality."

I got up and strode out the door to the jailhouse stable. I saddled up Warrior again, and he looked at me like, "Great. Let's go somewhere." We trotted out of town in a frisky state of mind.

* *

Toby Bodine and Allyson Miller sat in the kitchen speaking pleasantly of the new morning. The hurried clatter of a wagon and team broke the quiet. Suddenly an urgent rapping came at the door. Allyson rushed to the door. It was a young friend of hers, Trish Moulter, but she hardly recognized her.

Allyson stared at Trish. Her face was battered and bruised. One eye was swollen and half-way closed with a purple look. Her dress was tattered and dirty.

"Oh, Allyson! Pa did it again. He beat me something terrible, and then he turned on Ma when she tried to help me. I had to just about crawl out of the house. He is terribly mad angry, and I fear for Ma. Is there someone who can help us? Do you know someone who can help us?"

"Toby!" cried Allyson.

Toby Bodine stepped to the door. He took an instant look at the young sixteen year old and asked, "Who did this to you?" He already knew the answer.

"Pa did. He'd been drinking again and thinking about how our farm is failing. He blames us—Ma and me for his poor farming. He says that we brought him bad luck ever since I was born. They married young because Ma was with child. He's always felt that it was her fault that it happened. We've just got to get away from him, but he won't let us go. He told Ma that he would kill her if she left him. Please can we find someone to help us?"

Toby Bodine stayed quite calm despite the rise in his dander. He didn't hold with any man beating on a woman.

"Allyson, take your friend into the kitchen and do what you can for her. I'll be back in a few hours."

Toby saddled his dun and struck out toward the Moulter homestead. He arrived there some thirty minutes later.

A big rawboned man with gray-streaked dark hair and burly mustache stood in front of the ramshackle house saddling a buckskin horse. He turned and looked directly into the young Deputy Marshal's eyes. A cold feeling ran up Toby's spine. This man could be ugly mean. Toby had dealt with Moulter before about public drunkenness, but this situation was more serious.

"State yore business and then get offen my land," growled the man.

"I am Toby Bodine, Deputy U.S. Marshal. I am looking for Mrs. Moulter. I wish to talk to her."

"Yah. Well, she's my wife, and I don't cotton to her speaking with strangers, or anybody. A man's wife is his own property and of no business to anyone but her husband. Now, I said it once, I will say it for the last time. Get offen my land and leave us be."

Toby Bodine looked straight into the man's menacing dark brown eyes and said, "I came here to speak to Mrs. Moulter and I will not leave until I speak with her. Ask her to come out and speak with me. If you do not call her, I will. If you interfere with me in any way, I will arrest you. Now call her."

Jason Moulter's eyes flashed a distinct and ugly hatred look, but he turned and shouted loudly, "Woman! Get yourself out here! There's a stranger want's to speak with you."

Toby dismounted, turning the dun to keep it between him and Jason.

Jason's eyes flared at him again. If looks could kill, then Toby Bodine would have been in his grave.

A tall, frail-looking barefooted woman opened the door and slowly shuffled out into the dirt. She was shaking, and Toby could see the pain in her blue eyes. There was no mark on her face, but it was taunt with fear.

"Y-y-e-s?" she asked in a shaky and somewhat cracked voice. Her yes stayed looking at the ground.

Toby's eyes softened as he asked her, "Your daughter has told me of beatings. She's safe and staying with a friend. Did your husband beat your daughter and you? Do not be afraid to speak. I am the law here."

Clarice Moulter turned to look at her husband. Toby glanced at him out of the corner of his eye. The man's huge hands were clenched in tightened fists and his head cocked to one side. His eyes had narrowed to mere slits and he was staring at Clarice.

She answered with a complete nervousness, "Tain't none of your business, Marshal. I'm his woman, and our daughter has lied. My husband never beat on nobody. Please believe me. Go now. Tell Trish that I love her. Please go."

The woman turned slowly, and almost fell as she tried to step back through the door. She leaned against the doorframe for support, then slipped to the ground.

Toby Bodine immediately stepped forward to help and was confronted with the hulk of Jason Moulter. The man's huge hands moved to push Toby out of the way.

A blurr of the hand and suddenly, a cocked Colt Revolver stared Jason in the face. He stopped in mid-movement and slowly backed away. His hands were raised.

"On the ground, face down!" commanded Toby. The man did as ordered. The Deputy was young, but there was something in his eyes that told Jason he had better do as told.

Toby eased over to Clarice and knelt down beside her. She looked up at him with pain wracked and pleading eyes.

"Please, Marshal, go and leave us be. There can only be more trouble if you interfere."

"No, Mrs. Moulter. You need a doctor. I think that you have some broken ribs and God knows what else. I'm taking you into town and safety. You rest easy while your husband hitches up a team and wagon."

Thirty minutes later, Mrs. Moulter lay wrapped in blankets and lying in the bed of a ranch wagon. Jason Molter sat handcuffed to the hitching rack. Toby Bodine walked up to Jason and looked down upon him.

"I'm taking your wife into town to be seen by a Doctor. I know you beat her, and you beat your daughter also. Your wife will not file charges against you so I will not take you along."

Toby Bodine bent lower to Jason. He looked deeply into the man's eyes and said in a soft voice, "You have beat on them for the last time. If I ever hear of you beating them, or see a mark on either of them again, I will come here and personally beat you within an inch of your miserable life—badge or no badge."

Jason Moulter could only hang his head.

CHAPTER EIGHTEEN

"Dandy Jim Saunders"

Sheriff J. C. Kincaid watched lazily as the twice weekly stagecoach rumbled into town and rolled to a stop across the street from the jail. This was the most interesting time of the day. He got to see all of the new arrivals and he liked to try and guess what their business was. He watched as the passengers stepped out of the coach.

The last passenger out of the coach caused his blood to run cold.

There he stood, wearing the apparel that he had once called "my *working clothes.*" He was tall—about six foot one. He had dark hair, piercing dark eyes, and was clean shaved.

He wore a starched white shirt, cravat tie, fancy gold vest, and a dark suit. His highly shined, high topped black boots were adorned with silver roweled spurs.

Two nickel plated, bone handled Colt .44 Navy Revolvers hung low around his waist. It was said that he had killed over a dozen men in stand up gunfights. Rumor had it that others lay buried in lonely places all over the Southwest.

J.C. Kincaid could vouch for at least three of the face off gunfights. He had witnessed them.

A black, wide brimmed high-crowned Stetson set off the final touches to the man's ensemble. James *Dandy Jim* Saunders had arrived.

Dandy Jim's charm was like a magnet—drawing all manner of women to his side. Worst of all, though, a lot of two-bit gunmen who craved a reputation as a fast draw would be following him. Dandy Jim was a killer. A paid killer and his price was not cheap. Someone was going to die.

J.C. Kincaid was considered *handy* with a six-gun but not of the breed needed to face Saunders. Nevertheless, he followed Dandy Jim to the hotel where he watched him register for a room.

J.C. stood slightly behind and to the left. Saunders never looked up at the Sheriff, but spoke as he signed the register.

"Hello, J.C. Nice town you have here. I'll be here for a week—at most."

There it was. Dandy Jim Saunders would be in town for a week. He was there on business, of that, J.C. was sure. The only remaining question was—WHO was his business.

J.C. Kincaid sighed heavily. He was the only law within miles. U.S. Marshal Cole Stockton had ridden out to Creede. The Deputy Marshal Toby Bodine was also up in Creede. It would be days before either of them would return. He sorely wished that Cole Stockton had remained in town. He would know what to do about Dandy Jim.

* *

Laura Sumner wanted time to think.

Here she was, a young woman in her late twenties, and presumably attached somewhat to a middle-aged man. That there was an understandable *liking* between them was not to be denied.

Still, there was this feeling that she was missing something in life. She couldn't put her finger on it, but she knew that she had to put Cole Stockton out of her mind and her immediate life while she thought about it.

She saw the bewilderment in his eyes when she bid him to go, and she almost choked while she told him. She averted her eyes from his look, turned away, and told him to move into town.

His slamming of the front door angered her.

She had gone into the room he occupied and grabbed up everything that he owned. She had hesitated momentarily with the dark custom-made suit that she had given him for Christmas.

She remembered the dress that he had made the special trip to

Denver for. A slight mist came to her eyes. She almost wanted to run to him. To tell him that she was sorry. To tell him that she loved him.

"No," she said to herself. "I must do this for myself. I have to know and feel that it is right. That it truly is my destiny."

She carried Cole's few worldly possessions to the front door.

She saw him step up onto the porch, and she suddenly felt angry again. She felt confused. She didn't know what she felt.

She threw open the door of her house and threw all of his things out on to the porch. She saw the look on his face just before she slammed the door, and leaned back against it. Her mind raced. What did she do? Why did she do it? She stopped thinking and turned to look out the window.

Cole Stockton was riding away. He didn't knock on her door. He didn't call out to her. He just silently rode away. She watched until he was out of sight.

He never looked back. An hour passed before Laura understood that Cole wasn't returning anytime soon.

A sense of loneliness crawled silently into her mind and she felt a sudden chill. She shivered slightly.

A knock at the front door interrupted her momentary thoughts. She peeked out and there stood Judd Ellison.

Judd stood at the door, Cole's folded suit in his hands. He was somber looking. She opened the door and said, "Come in, Judd. You look like something is on your mind. What is it?"

Judd handed the suit to Laura. Her eyes widened in surprise. She took it with slightly trembling hands and laid it on the sofa.

"Miss Laura, can I speak freely?"

"Yes, Judd. I've always listened to you. You know I always listen to your advice. I may not take it all the time, but I will listen."

"I heard tell that you told Cole to leave and move into town. I saw the look on his face when he left and it was mighty sorrowful. I've know'd you two for quite some time now, and I have the utmost respect for the both of you. You know that. Iffen it were something he did, maybe it is for the best but, pardon my thoughts, it was wrong sending him away like that. Things can always be worked out with some soulful talking. Miss Laura, it was wrong. I guess that's all I have to say."

"Thank you, Judd. It's something that I have to work out on my own. I appreciate your thoughts."

"Shucks, Miss Laura, we—the boys and I just want you to be happy. You are about the best boss we ever worked for, and when the chips are down, we will do what is necessary to set it right. Well, I got to see to Sultan. He has been acting mighty frisky lately, and I think its about time to put them mares with him. What do you think?"

"Yes, Judd. It is time. Sultan is the beginning of a great line of horses. Think of it. A horse ranch with the MOST beautifully well-bred horses in the area. It's everything I've ever dreamed about. Please see to it."

* *

Laura Sumner felt a curious longing. "Well, I do have to ride into town and pick up a few things at the general store. I'll just drop in at the hotel and see if Cole is registered there. Not that it matters, but somehow I want to know."

An hour later found Laura entering the hotel. She stepped up to the desk behind Sheriff Kincaid and a well-dressed *gentleman* of about twenty-eight. The gentleman turned suddenly and their eyes met.

Laura felt the penetrating gaze as it seemingly warmed her senses. She smiled at the man. He looked interesting, and he was handsome, not to mention that he was around her age.

The man smiled back at her with great appreciation.

"Well, now, J.C., you didn't tell me that such beauty resided in the midst of this wild and desolate land. Should I be lost in heaven? For I have just encountered an angel. Tell me most lovely woman, what is your name?"

J.C. Kincaid swallowed hard. He couldn't believe it. There was Laura Sumner, almost giddy, wide-eyed, and looking at Dandy Jim Saunders like he was an ancient Grecian god.

"I am Laura—Laura Sumner. I own a horse ranch about an hour's ride from town. And who are you?"

"Why, my enchanted one—I am James Saunders. I am only traveling through this forsaken country. I come from hither and always travel to yon, but never in my most miserable life have I met such a vision of loveliness. Surely, you are a dream, and I dread to wake from it. You must have dinner with me—tonight. What is your most favorite restaurant in this poor excuse for a town? We will partake of only the best. It is the least I can do to pay homage to the aura of beauty that surrounds you."

Laura laughed gaily at his boldness. Never in her life had she been so swept off her feet than at this very moment. She took James Saunders' offered arm, and out to the street they went.

J.C. Kincaid stood there just shaking his head.

"I can't believe it, Laura Sumner, of all people. Just wait until Cole Stockton hears about this. There will be Hell to pay."

Suddenly, it dawned on him. There was one man in all of the entire Lower Colorado Territory that stood between the factions of lawlessness and peace—Cole Stockton. The Sheriff now knew WHO Dandy Jim's business was, and an icy shiver ran up his spine.

* *

Laura Sumner sat across the table from James Saunders. She ignored the curious stares of townsfolk who knew who she was but didn't know her escort. He was exciting to her. He spoke with such eloquence. She sensed that he was deliberately charming her, but she didn't care. He was fun to be with. He was like a breath of fresh air to her.

Laura, for all her learning, had failed to notice the manner in which James Saunders wore his guns. She had momentarily glanced at the bone-handled Colts but immediately reverted her gaze to his winning smile and her ears to his poetic phrases.

She was all ears to his smooth conversation. He seemed versed on everything from the most modern ladies fashions to the most interesting stories and fiction of the day. He knew funny jokes. He laughed a lot. There was a certain gleam in his eye, and Laura believed that the gleam was for her.

At one point during the dinner, Laura almost caught a fleeting passage from her late Uncle Jesse's words.

"A man is sometimes not what he seems to be."

She passed it off as she laughed while James Saunders told another funny story.

* *

The trail to Creede was long and wound upward through wondrous mountain passes. At one point, I sighed heavily, then turned Warrior up a slope well off the trail. I seemed to want to think things through, for whatever sense I could make of it. I dismounted about a hundred yards up, and just sat there listening to the wind blow through the pines and aspen. I'd felt empty on times before, but it was nothing compared to the weight on my mind now.

"What if," I asked myself, "what if, she NEVER wanted to see me again? What if, I could NEVER hold her hand, or gaze longingly into her eyes?"

That word NEVER was chillingly cold to my soul, and I shivered a bit.

Warrior nudged me with his head.

"O.K. I got the message. It was time to move on. I got up from the ground and stretched. It was still a long way to Creede, and if I was going to make it by midnight, I had to travel. Still—it was not urgent that I get there soon.

I decided to lazily work my way along the trail, and once again my thoughts drifted back to Laura.

She was young and vibrant. I was a trail-hardened member of the *Clan of the Gun*. I was a fool to even think that I could amount to anything worthwhile in her eyes.

The more I thought about it, the less I thought of myself.

Finally, I pulled Warrior up abruptly. I touched my Colt and a shiver ran up my spine. I glanced down at the Silver Star on my vest.

"It just marks the target," I said softly to myself. "Perhaps that is all I am good for—a target."

I clucked to Warrior and we again moved forward at our slow wandering pace.

Suddenly, a thunderously loud RUMBLE! Tons of earth, rock, and ripped up trees came sliding down the mountainside—right at us.

I looked up the slope and it was as if the whole mountain was coming straight down on us. I sunk spur to Warrior and he jumped as if the very Devil himself was on our heels.

Dust, rock, dirt, parts of trees, and every part of holy creation came down on us. It doesn't take much in the mountains. Bad weather with lots of rain, erosion sets in—all of a sudden—a minute chip slips somewhere, a rock rolls into another rock, and pretty soon trees are uprooted, and down it comes.

I leaned hard forward in the saddle as I felt that young chestnut's muscles spring hard and fast. The thunder of that landslide was deafening. Dirt and rocks flew everywhere.

The Almighty, Himself, must have been looking out for us because we just barely outran the edge of that hundred-yards-or-so turmoil.

Small bits and pieces of the slide were still sweeping under Warrior's feet when we reached the far side of that tumultuous movement.

When we were fully clear, I pulled up sharp. My heart thumped wildly. I fairly jumped out of the saddle and threw my arms around Warrior's neck. I hugged that horse like he was my brother.

"Remind me to get you something special when we get to Creede," I promised. I knew he would.

That slide, nature's unpredictable action, reminded me that I'd better keep my senses about me while traveling through this area. Being lost in thought about a woman is one thing, having immediate danger shout at you with an instant warning is another.

"Cole Stockton," I said to myself "If you're not careful, you could get yourself killed."

How ironic that seemed! I had faced in my time, close to a hundred men, including various Indians, bent on taking my life in one fashion or another. To be lying dead under a couple of tons of dirt would be folly. I knew better.

I had ridden these trails long enough to know that one slip in the wilds and a man would die a lonely death. There is no one but fate or destiny to keep it otherwise. Although not a regular church-going man, I silently thanked the Lord for his quick thinking and kind regard for my well-being.

Looking back at the slide I saw that a dirt cloud still hung heavy in the air. I would pass the word when I reached Creede. They would send out a passel of men, mules, and mining equipment to clear the pass.

Another five miles or so later, it was nearing dusk, when Warrior's ears suddenly pricked up. I listened carefully. Then I heard it. It sounded like a baby crying.

CHAPTER NINETEEN

"Sheriff Kincaid's Dilemma"

Toby Bodine reached into his jeans pocket and produced the key to the handcuffs that held Jason Moulter to the hitching rack. He bent down and unlocked the first shackle. Jason suddenly reared up and threw his large bulk firmly against the young Deputy. Toby flew backward to land on his back in the dust. Moulter lunged toward him with a burning vengeance in his eyes.

Bodine's hand flashed to his holster. A quick blur and the Colt fluidly swept up, cocked and ready, pointed right at Jason's middle. Jason stopped in mid-stride, but he glared at Bodine and snarled, "I'm going to get you for this, you young whelp. I'm going to get you good."

Bodine glared back at the man.

"Anytime—<u>after</u> I see to your wife's welfare. In the meantime, you just back off before I am forced to shoot you. Don't ever try to jump me again."

Bodine got to his feet and somewhat dusted himself off. He kept the Colt trained on Jason until he was situated in the wagon seat and started the team into motion. He heard Jason shouting threats at him as he drove the wagon towards the town of Creede.

* *

J.C. Kincaid stood on the boardwalk outside the town's only fine restaurant. He watched through the window while James Saunders continued to fascinate Laura Sumner with his suave manner and good looks.

"I guess nothing will happen tonight," he thought "Think I will go down to the Lady Luck and have a cool beer."

He turned and strode purposely to the batwing doors.

Louise Montrose stood near the piano singing a sorrowful tune about a lost and lonesome love. Her eyes followed J.C. to the bar.

Louise finished the song, and then tossed her hanky into the air. A half dozen lonely men scrambled for the perfumed souvenir. It was a bearded old man that caught it and clutched it to his chest like it was worth a ton of gold. To him it was.

Louise waved and smiled at the crowd of men, who rose to their feet, clapped loudly, and tried to coerce her into another song. She audibly announced to the crowd that she would return within a half-hour and sing a few requested songs. The men reluctantly nodded their heads while they clapped their approval.

Louise made her way to the bar and stood beside the Sheriff.

"Howdy, J.C.," she said, "town kind of quiet tonight?"

"It is for the moment, Louise, for the moment."

"J.C., Cole Stockton was in here earlier this morning. He sure looked like he'd lost his best friend. What's going on?"

"W-e-l-l," replied Kincaid, "it seems that there was some kind of tiff between Cole and Laura Sumner. Laura made Cole leave the ranch. That's only the half of it. There's a man arrived in town today. A hired killer. Name's—Saunders—"Dandy Jim" Saunders. Right now, Laura Sumner and Saunders are having dinner at the Palace restaurant, and she appears to be having a great time."

Louise cocked her head a bit and inquired, "Does Miss Sumner know about this man?"

"No, I don't believe she does. Maybe she don't want to know. I sure ain't going to be the one to tell her right now either. Damn, I wish that Cole was here. Saunders is very highly paid for his work and I fear that Cole may be his next job."

Louise's heart thumped wildly. She had a soft spot in her heart for Cole Stockton, but she also knew that as long as Laura was on his mind, there was no way that she would be noticed. After all, who was she? She was a part saloon owner, fairly good singer, but not a woman of enviable reputation.

Louise Montrose had left the East, at the tender age of seventeen, with illusions of finding a husband and a solid future in the West. Instead, she initially found herself attached for a few years, to a slick-talking gambler who got killed over a bad game of cards.

She had no money to speak of and she had to survive. She turned to the only thing that she could do. Her striking five foot six figure, auburn hair, and dreamy brown eyes were such that men took notice, and she could read the desire in their eyes. They were willing to pay.

She hustled drinks in saloons, sang a few songs, and spent the night with a few *select* customers. Over a span of ten years, she had finally saved up enough money to buy a half interest in the Lady Luck Saloon.

Colorado was filled with rough men, and Louise learned quickly to read a man's makeup by his eyes and by the way he wore a gun. She could spot a problem fairly quick and, because of such, quelled a lot of trouble before it happened. Men learned to respect her, and she learned to respect them for what they were—MEN. She also became established as a tolerated business woman in the eyes of the local *Ladies Society*.

Her mind reflected back to the look that Cole Stockton had given her that morning. He had looked fairly straight into her eyes, and it was like he had finally noticed her—for the first time.

Stockton was the only lawman that she could recall who treated her like a lady. She felt as if he held a respect for any woman of the West, no matter what her profession, or background. It was a feeling that she cherished.

Although she knew many men, there were only a few that kindled the fires of her very soul. Cole Stockton was one of those few.

Just now, hearing J.C. Kincaid's words, she felt a foreboding shudder run through her body. She had heard of Dandy Jim Saunders and the word passed around was that there was "no one faster or better." She feared for Cole Stockton's life.

* *

It was well on toward midnight when Laura Sumner suddenly realized that she should be going. She smiled at James Saunders with brightly gleaming eyes and said, "It's late. I should have departed hours ago. The ride to my ranch is about an hour long, and I've things that I must do tomorrow. Please excuse me."

James Saunders, being the gentleman that he sometimes portrayed, and knowing the dangers of a night ride in wild territory, spoke.

"Nonsense, Laura. What true-blooded gentleman would allow a lady of your obvious beauty to ride wild trails in the shadow of nightfall? There is no moon this eve and I fear that your ride may be perilous. You shall stay here—in town—at the hotel, in accommodations befitting a queen. I have detained you and feel responsible for your well-being. Allow me, please, to redeem myself—to redeem my honor as a gentleman. I will have it no other way. You WILL be my guest."

Laura Sumner was enthralled. Here was a true gentleman. He offered his arm once again, and she took it. They marched to the hotel, and James Saunders hailed the night clerk to "Provide a room befitting the Queen of the Universe."

The room, by coincidence, just happened to be across the hall from James Saunders.

* *

Toby Bodine rode steadily through the night. He had driven the wagon to Creede, and stayed with the Doctor and Mrs. Moulter until the story was unraveled. Mrs. Moulter had seven broken ribs, several discolored bruises all over her body, and a fractured left arm. Now he would see the daughter Trish again and advise of her mother's situation and care.

He pulled up at the hitching rack and dismounted. A lamp burned only in the kitchen window. He rapped lightly at the door. Allyson Miller opened the door, then rushed into his arms. He held her tightly. She lifted her face to him and they kissed.

"How is Trish?" he asked.

"She is sleeping soundly in my bed. She has bruises all over her body, and her face is swollen, but she is young and will be all right in a few days. You were gone so long. How is Mrs. Moulter?"

Toby replied, "She was beaten badly. I can surmise that this is not the first time. I left her at the doctor's office in town. We need to find somewhere that they can stay for a few days. I looked into Mr. Moulter's eyes, and there is a burning hatred. He is on the edge of madness, and I fear for both of their lives."

"Toby" said Allyson, "I've already spoken to Mother and Father. They can stay here with us. You be careful. I have only met that man once or twice, but he is very dangerous. I sensed that from the very first."

"Don't worry, Allyson. I can take care of myself. Now, how about a cup of that good strong coffee? Maybe a sandwich or so, I haven't eaten anything since those biscuits and jam this morning."

Allyson looked at Toby Bodine with inviting eyes. "Are you sure that's ALL you want? Maybe I could use a little bit of spooning tonight. A young woman has got to know that that someone cares for her."

* *

J.C. Kincaid finished his third beer. He looked at Louise Montrose and thought about how it might be if, he were able to support a family. He thought about his dream. He thought about having a nice wife, a nice little ranch, a couple of children, and a bit of money to make things comfortable.

He had taken this sheriff job because it paid a bit more than wrangling horses or *punching* steers. Each of those jobs was hard work, and although he didn't mind hard work, he had more of a knack for the gun. He was considered good but not of the speed and proficiency as Cole Stockton, Wyatt Earp, or James Butler Hickok, or half a dozen other known men. Yet, there was a certain decency about him.

Fifty dollars a month, feed and found, and all the bullets he needed was good pay to J.C. That meant forty dollars a month for him, feed for his horse, anything "found" such as fines, rewards for wanted persons, free meals at the town's restaurant or café, citizens homes, or whatever else he deemed necessary in the performance of his duties as Town Sheriff. His jurisdiction ended at the edge of town. He didn't want to go out in the wilds and hunt down any bad men anyway. That was the County Sheriff, Territorial Marshal, or U.S. Marshal's job.

If he did take a prisoner, it was up to the U.S. Marshal to escort the prisoner to justice at the nearest court. All J.C. Kincaid had to do was keep the peace, and right now he wished that he were a better man.

If he were more bold, if he were better with a gun, if he were more handsome, if, if, if; maybe Louise would look at him with more than a passing smile and a "Good Morning, J.C."

He was quite taken by her charms, and the thought was always in the back of his mind "There are over a hundred men who would give their lives for Louise. A lot of them are handsome. A lot of them have more means of support. A lot of them talk better than me. Ah, what's the use? She'll never notice me."

CHAPTER TWENTY

"Cole Stockton's Demise"

I listened intently. There it was again. There was a baby crying in the wilds. What direction was it? I listened again. My next thought was "Give Warrior the lead." I did.

Warrior moved forward, then around the next bend. His ears pricked up again, and then he turned up a steep slope. We climbed until the incline was so steep that I had to dismount. I continued to follow Warrior up the slope, holding on to his tail.

Finally, we topped out over a rim to find a lone broken down ranch wagon. A thin-looking man was pointing a shotgun at me. A short slightly-plump, blonde woman and two small children sat around a small campfire behind him. A baby nestled in her arms.

"Who or what ya be?" he asked.

"U.S. Marshal," I announced.

The man looked closer at me and squinted slightly. Rather, he looked closer at the Silver Star on my vest.

"Come closer, I want to see you in the light."

I moved a bit closer to the fire. He concentrated on the badge, then suddenly nodded. He lowered the shotgun.

"Marshal, we was headed to Creede when our wagon broke down up here in the middle of nowhere. I got no way to fix it and no money to pay to fix it. I had to shoot one of the horses. It broke its leg when the wagon axle snapped. We's just here. I don't know what to do other than just sit here until someone comes along and helps. There ain't nobody passed across this route for the past three days. I'm sorry about the shotgun, but we was told to trust nobody in the wilds—especially at night."

"Good advice," I replied. "Just who are you?"

"Name's Clarence Bundy. This here is my family. Well, let's see. We broke down about three days ago. Our water is running mighty low. We've no more canned milk for the baby. Loretta has given her teat, and now she has dried up."

These folks were in a heap of trouble. More trouble than they knew. I couldn't help thinking that this was summer 1879 and there were still some renegade Indian factions out here. I tried not to think about the possibility of this family's scalps hanging on a Ute or Southern Cheyenne Warrior's lance. It was also not within me to mention some white men who would kill at the drop of a hat and take all they could—even the woman.

I looked at the two small children and the baby.

"When was the last time you had anything to eat?"

"Been about a day, Marshal. We got coffee, flour, sugar, and a bit of beans. That's all."

"Well," I said, "The first thing is to get some food. I have a small packet of beef jerky, and a few hard biscuits. I have two canteens of water. You have coffee—I like it strong and black. You have beans. Grab a pot and let's make a trail supper of beef and beans. I could sure use a good cup of coffee right now."

I looked at the children and they managed a slight smile. The young boy—about eight years old seemed fascinated with my revolver. I suddenly thought back to my younger years along the West Texas and New Mexico plains and my own pa. There were Comanche raids then, and a lot of scavengers, too. The scavengers came to the West from the War that was raging in the East. They were dodging the military and living off the fat of the land. What they wanted, they took.

I remember that I was ten years old when my pa took me out to the back fence and told me straight out, "Bobby Cole, there may come a time when I may not be here. It is up to you to be the man of the house. I'm gonna teach you to shoot. I want you to be the best that you can. It's time you was a young man instead of a child. Can you do it?"

"Yes, Pa. I'll try. I will be the best with the gun that I can be."

"O.K., Bobby Cole, I'll put six tins on the fence. I will shoot two of them. You will watch me and then, I want you to shoot the other four."

That was a long time ago, but I remember it like it was yesterday. Suddenly, I smelled coffee brewing. It was like a breath of fresh air, renewing my senses, and telling me that if these folks were to be saved, I was the one that had to do it. I once again glanced down upon the Silver Star pinned to my vest.

"I wonder if I am worthy of it?" I asked myself.

* *

Laura Sumner shut the door of her hotel room that James Saunders insisted he pay for, and slowly took it in. The room was quite elegant for this town. She readied herself for bed, and as she turned out the oil lamp and lay her head on the pillow, her thoughts turned to the events of the day.

She had told Cole Stockton to go that morning. She had thrown his possessions out on the porch and she watched him ride away. She remembered that he hadn't even looked back.

"Why didn't he look back?" she wondered "He must not love me like he said that he did. If he really loved me, he would've looked back."

She thought about why she decided to check for him at the hotel.

"Why did I go to check on him? I don't know. It was something that I just felt that I had to do."

Laura drifted off to sleep thinking of Cole Stockton. She dreamt of shaking ground and sliding boulders. She almost felt choking dust in her throat and her heart was pounding.

Laura woke up in a cold sweat. Why did she feel this way? Was the dream an omen?

* *

Dandy Jim Saunders readied himself for bed. He placed one of his revolvers under his pillow, turned down the oil lamp, and lay there in the darkness staring at the ceiling.

He had come to this town with a mission—a deadly mission. The newly resurrected Association had paid him good money to take on Cole Stockton. They wanted him out of the way very badly.

Luck was with him, he thought, "I've only been here a few hours and already I've met and charmed Stockton's woman. He seems to be out on the trail somewhere, but he will be back and when he sees me with Laura, he will be extremely jealous. He will make a mistake, and I will kill him. I can't wait to see the look on his face."

And then he thought, "Too bad about Laura. At a different time and place, I could really go for this woman myself. She is a real looker."

* *

Sheriff J.C. Kincaid rose early, looked out the jail window, and was surprised to see that the stagecoach to Creede was still at the stage depot. It normally departed around seven in the morning.

He dressed, then walked to the depot where he found Jeb Mason, the stationmaster.

"Hey, Jeb. How come the stage to Creede ain't left yet?"

"Morning, J.C. The stage can't go. Whit Runlee came through early this morning, and there's been a landslide that blocked the whole road. Only enough room for a horse and rider to get through the pass. It will be days before it is cleared off. And that ain't all. He checked the area and there is horse tracks leading into the slide, but nothing coming out on the other side."

J.C. suddenly thought of Cole Stockton.

"Did Whit happen to mention seeing Marshal Stockton on the trail. He should have passed him."

"No. He said that he saw no one on the trail."

Immediately, J.C. Kincaid started to worry.

"I wonder if Cole made it through that landslide? I'll have that old Indian, John Running Calf, go and have a look."

* *

I camped out with the Bundy family until day break.

"Time to get moving," I said, and helped the woman and baby up on the remaining wagon team horse. I had the other two children up on Warrior. I slung my Winchester and canteens over my shoulder and Bundy carried his shotgun along with a pack with what provisions he could muster up.

We began the trek to Creede. It would take us about a day and a half traveling like this. That is, unless someone came along with a wagon, and I sorely wished that someone would. I knew also that there was no way that a wagon could get through the pass from my direction. The only hope was that someone would be coming in a wagon from the Creede way.

We trekked for half a day, stopping only to rest for an hour at a time. The children seemed to be having a great time riding on Warrior, and he seemed to like them also.

In the late afternoon, I spotted them. A cavalry detachment of about a dozen troopers was riding parallel to us and about a quarter mile away. I shucked my Winchester and quickly fired three rounds into the air. That got their attention, and they came a riding to us.

They were out of Fort Lyon and were heading towards Creede also. We split the Bundy family to double up on the cavalry horses. It looked like I would get into Creede sometime that evening.

* *

Toby Bodine left the Miller farm in the early afternoon. He wanted to drop in on Mrs. Moulter at Doc Wilson's office to see how she was doing.

Once he arrived at the doctor's office, he found the door slightly ajar. Stepping inside, he immediately saw the doctor lying on the floor, unconscious.

A creak sounded behind him, and as he turned, he saw the hulk of Jason Moulter—just before the axe handle hit him across the left side.

Bodine grunted with the sharp crack. He knew that at least some of his ribs were broken. Again the axe handle was wielded, and Toby slammed to the floor. Mouter continued to beat on Toby with the wooden handle until the young Deputy passed out.

"Told you I'd get you good," growled Jason.

Then he turned toward the door, dropped the axe handle, went out the door, got into his wagon and drove out of town. He intended to leave this here territory and go to New Mexico. He was taking his wife and leaving. His ungrateful daughter, Trish, could fend for herself. He would settle with his wife later. She was the cause of all of his bad luck, and she would pay for it with her life. He could hide her body in the mountains and then disappear to start a new life somewhere.

* *

John Running Calf dismounted at the landslide site. He was following Warrior's tracks. He had stopped by the jailhouse stable and studied Warrior's hoof prints. He found it easy to follow Cole Stockton's trail right up to the point that the landslide covered the road.

"Stock-Ton was in big earth slide," he thought to himself. He surveyed the scene carefully.

"No one escape this much dirt. This much rock coming down that fast. Maybe Stock-Ton buried in dirt. I will check the other side."

The old Indian tracker rode warily through the narrow passage left in the aftermath. He saw the tracks of Whit Runlee's horse coming from the Creede direction. But there were no other tracks in the passageway. He reached the other side of the slide and examined the ground. He found no tracks leading away from the slide. He pondered the situation. To him, Cole Stockton was buried under all that earth. He raised his face and arms toward the sun and began an old Indian death chant. Mar-shal Stock-Ton was dead, and he would pass the news.

* *

Laura Sumner stayed in town rather than return to her ranch that morning. She stood in the hotel lobby speaking pleasantly with James

Saunders when a grim faced J.C. Kincaid approached them. He held his hat in his hand, something that J.C. rarely did.

Laura glanced away from Saunders for an instant to meet with J.C.'s red rimmed and somber eyes.

"Laura," he began, "I don't know how to tell you this, and I sure wish that I didn't have to be the one. You better sit down over there in that chair."

Laura, James Saunders, and Sheriff Kincaid moved to a chair along the wall. Laura sat down, and looked questioningly up at J.C.

"O.K., I'm seated. What is it, J.C.?"

J.C. Kincaid swallowed hard. He wished that he were somewhere else than standing in front of Laura Sumner with this solemn news.

"Cole Stockton is dead. He happened into the middle of a landslide that took out almost the entire road in the passes between here and Creede. I sent John Running Calf out to check the scene, and he found Cole's tracks going into the slide, but there was nothing come out the other side of all that dirt and rock. Cole Stockton is buried under tons of earth. We may never find his body."

Laura's face went ashen. Her eyes widened in disbelief. Her heart seemed to jump right up into her throat and she couldn't speak. She closed her eyes and her dream of tons of moving earth rushed to the forefront of her mind.

James Saunders moved beside her. He reached down and gently took her hands in his. He pulled her up and the bewildered Laura moved hypnotically into his arms. Laura buried her face against his shoulder and sobbed. Saunders tried to calm her by lightly touching her hair and holding her tight. He whispered calming phrases into her ear.

Laura looked up at James Saunders with tear-filled eyes. He looked into her sorrowful eyes and brushed away her tears on her cheek. She halfheartedly pushed away from him, but he kept a firm hold on her.

Laura's head was spinning. She spoke in disbelief. "Cole—dead? Cole Stockton is dead? He can't be dead. He just can't be dead. Not after all we have been through together. He can't be dead."

"Yes, Laura." Saunders responded, "Cole Stockton is dead. Didn't you hear what J.C. said, the Indian tracker said that Cole Stockton is dead. He is dead and buried under tons of earth and debris."

Laura Sumner collapsed against James Saunders. He wrapped his arms around her, holding her firmly. A sly smile spread slowly across Dandy Jim's face.

CHAPTER TWENTY-ONE

"Jason Moulter"

The cavalry detachment, the Bundy family, and I arrived in Creede around eight that night. I saw to the Bundy family, making introductions at one of the local hotels. The owner of the hotel owed me a favor and as such allowed the family to stay in a room for a couple of nights—free of charge.

I also stopped by Sam and Sarah's Café, which was right next door and spoke with the couple who ran it. They both seemed to like helping folks in need, and I gave them money to cover meals.

I had a cup of their fine coffee with Sam at a small table by the back wall when Will Johnson, Creede's Deputy Sheriff walked in.

"Cole! Marshal Stockton. When did you get in? Toby Bodine has been hurt real bad. Some wild man beat him with an axe handle and he is broke up something fierce. You got to go and see him. He has been asking for us to find you. We telegraphed but the lines must be down between here and there. He is at the doctor's hospital at the hotel."

I thanked the young deputy for the information and hurried down the street to the doctor's hospital space.

Toby Bodine lay in a bed close to one of the windows. I approached him slowly and stood beside him. My heart went out to my friend.

Toby looked up at me with hazy eyes. The doctor had sedated him, but he was still aware of who he was. He smiled at me with swollen face.

"Hello Cole. Glad you could make it."

"Who did this to you, Toby?" I asked.

He told me the story. I had met Jason on one occasion and I didn't like him then, and I sure as Hell didn't like him now.

Just then, the Creede town Sheriff, Jerrod Tulley walked in.

"Will Johnson told me that you were here, Cole. I found out that Jason Moulter drove his wagon out of here just a few hours ago. It looked like he was headed south. I don't have jurisdiction to go after him, or I would have. He should be on the road somewhere between here and the Lower Colorado."

"That's O.K., Jerrod. I'll go and get him. Besides, he can't make it through the pass with a wagon. There was a landslide and the pass is blocked. Send some men and mining equipment up there as soon as you can." Jerrod looked surprised at the news and nodded that he understood.

I turned to Toby.

"Rest easy, Son. I will get this man, or die trying."

As an afterthought, I put on my silly grin and said, "By the way— take the next couple of days off."

Toby was hurting, but he laughed anyway. I knew he would make out all right. Besides, Allyson would be by his side, of that I was sure.

I hitched up Warrior, and lit out down the road for the Lower Colorado. I wanted this man, Jason, and the more I thought about it, the madder I got.

* *

J.C. Kincaid shuffled slowly into the Lady Luck Saloon. His eyes caught Louise Montrose in a direct line, and she quickly stepped up to him.

"J.C., I've never seen you look like this. Is something wrong? What is it? Maybe I can help."

Kincaid looked her directly in the eye.

"I'm afraid that Cole Stockton is dead. There was a huge landslide up in the passes between here and Creede. Cole's tracks lead into the slide, but they do not come out on the other side. It looks like he is buried under tons of earth and we may never find his body."

Louise stepped back, wide-eyed, her hand to her breasts.

"No! Cole can't be dead. Not like that. He's traveled those passes.

He knows the dangers. I can't believe it. I refuse to believe it." Louise's distress drew the attention of everyone in the saloon. Something terrible had happened.

"Louise. It is the truth. I sent John Running Calf to check for signs of Cole. He told me that Cole Stockton is dead and buried under that avalanche. I believe him. Marshal Stockton is dead. Anyway, there will be a service for him at the church the day after tomorrow at three in the afternoon. I just thought that you might like to know."

J.C. Kincaid caught the look in Louise's eyes and suddenly knew her feelings for Cole Stockton. He turned abruptly and with a heavy heart walked out the saloon's doors.

Louise stared after him. Suddenly she recognized the hurt look in J.C.'s eyes. J.C. had been in love with her for years. She began to think about all those times when J.C. Kincaid was around her. There were little things, a smile, a glance, a kind remark here and there. She thought about her own loneliness. She thought about J.C. Kincaid and her—together.

* *

Laura Sumner found herself back at the hotel room. She only vaguely recalled being helped up the stairs. She stared at the walls around her. She could not believe it! Cole Stockton was dead? She didn't want to believe it, but everything pointed to it as the truth.

What would she do? Cole had been part of her very soul ever since she first arrived in the Lower Colorado. There was a magnetic attraction between them. They could look deeply into each other's eyes and read them. They could feel what each other was feeling. She felt very empty inside-and lonely.

She looked at the bed and felt very tired. There was emptiness in her heart. She must rest and think this through, so she readied herself for bed.

Laura dreamed while she fitfully slept. She dreamed of her old friend, Maude Pritchard. Maude seemed to be telling her something, and the words formed before her eyes.

"You will have to decide your destiny. There is one who will stoke the fires of your soul. He is born of a deadly skill, but you will seek the comfort of his honor. There will be LOVE."

Maude faded from her nocturnal vision.

A new vision formed. It was a man on a dark-colored chestnut horse. The man's face was darkened and she couldn't see it. He was riding hard. The horse was seemingly stretched out in an all out run for life. There was an aura surrounding them, a multicolored aura that resembled a raging fire.

The vision faded.

Another vision formed. A huge, evil-looking figure loomed up and was walking steadily toward another unrecognized figure. They grappled. They were beating each other severely. They rolled toward a cliff. They were going to fall over the edge into empty space. A woman screamed.

Laura Sumner woke up and stared into the darkness. She was the woman who was screaming. Her heart was pounding. She was wet with sweat and she was breathless.

A rapid pounding came at the door, and she called out, "Who is it?"

"James Saunders. Are you all right? I heard a scream."

Laura quickly pulled a blanket to cover herself and answered through the door. "I am fine. I just had a bad dream. I will be all right. Please leave me alone. I'll be fine."

Saunders retreated to his own room and Laura Sumner fell back against her pillow—exhausted. She slept again, and this time she dreamed of Cole Stockton riding toward her. At that point, her mind knew. Cole Stockton was alive. He was alive and was on his way back to her.

She pulled her pillow close to her breast and it felt warm. She snuggled against it and drifted into a peaceful slumber.

* *

Warrior and I rode hard in the direction of the Lower Colorado wilds. Jason had a good head start, and I wanted to catch up with him quickly.

Riding alone gives a man the time to think. I was thinking hard. Not about Laura this time, but about my young deputy. This Jason feller was awful-to-the-bone mean, and I was going to repay him for what he had done.

It was around early dawn when I spotted the wagon. It was pulled off the road a bit and upon checking it out, the wagon was empty. I looked around and found some rather large and deep shoe imprints. Those prints looked to be farmer's footwear rather than the boots that riders would wear. I followed them up through a winding ravine.

The ravine wound around and went up slope for about fifty yards. A slight wind was blowing, and I thought I heard muffled crying. It sounded a lot like someone, a woman maybe, was pleading with someone. The crying was followed by a deeper voice telling her to go ahead and scream.

As I crept closer, the conversation became all too clear. "There is no one to hear you up here in the passes! Go ahead and scream loud! I want you to scream! I want to hear you scream as I choke and beat the life out of you! Scream, dammit!"

I drew my Colt and rushed up to the crest. As I topped over, I saw them. The woman was bound hand and foot. The man held her by the front of her tattered dress and then he hit her. He hit her in the face with his big meaty fist, and I could hear the ugly splat. He drew back his fist again and that's when I fired a shot into the air. He jerked up and turned toward me. His face was distorted by ugly meanness and his eyes stared crazy wild.

"U.S. Marshal! Leave the woman be. You are under arrest for beating on this woman, and also for the beating and attempted murder of Deputy U.S. Marshal Toby Bodine. You will come peaceably or I will shoot you and leave your dead carcass for the scavengers."

He looked at me with those wild eyes and scowled.

"Go ahead and shoot, Marshal. I can wring her miserable neck before you can get to me, and then I'll come and get you before I die."

He had a point there, and I believed him. I holstered my Colt. I reached up and took off my star and pinned it to my holster. Then, I unbuckled my gunbelt and let it slip to the ground.

"O.K., Jason. I owe you anyway. I'm going to give you what you deserve, and then I will haul your hurt and bleeding carcass back to answer at Judge Wilkerson's court."

He looked at me with surprise-widened eyes. A big crooked evil grin broke over his hate-twisted face and he dropped the woman. He started toward me, laughing.

He was laughing because he stood taller and he outweighed me by at least eighty pounds. He was Almighty-sure of himself.

He planned to take this skinny Marshal and whop him good. He was going to kill me with his bare hands, and I knew that he could do it.

We both went into a crouch. He lunged at me and I sidestepped him to the right. He fell face down on the hard rocky ground. He was quick for a big man, though, and he got up fast, turning on me again. His face was bleeding where it scraped on rocks.

He lunged at me again. This time I sidestepped to the left and swung a fist straight into the side of his face as he hurled past me. I felt his neck jerk with the impact of that hit. He

slumped to the ground, but like before, jumped up and onto his feet, then rushed me again.

I wasn't as fast this time, and he slammed into me, bowling us both over. We grappled for leverage. He got one big hand around my left wrist and was bending it. His other arm was around my body and he was trying to squeeze the life out of me.

I got my right hand around his throat and squeezed with all the strength I could muster. He gurgled and released my left wrist. I quickly withdrew my right hand from his throat and as his hands went to his neck, I slammed him in the gut with my knee. He doubled up as I rolled away trying to catch my breath.

I got to my feet and saw that Jason was just coming to his knees. I rushed up to him and jammed a knee into his bleeding face. He jerked back like he was hit with a sledge hammer. I moved to him and grabbed his shirt front, pulling him up to a sitting position.

"Come on, Moulter, I'm not through with you yet."

I pulled him to his feet, and he suddenly came alive with a second wind burst of high energy. He lunged into me and we both went tumbling to the ground and rolled over and over and over.

I slammed him in the face and stomach several times as hard as I could. I was madder than Hell and I wanted to beat him into submission. He was also slamming me hard and I could feel the power of his blows to my mid-section. I hurt like Hell.

I hurt like Hell, but I was too damn mad and miserable to let it bother me. I was getting tired now, and knew that it had to end pretty fast or Jason would get the best of me.

He slammed me hard in the face, and I spit blood from a split lip. The taste of my own blood just angered me even more, and suddenly— all the pent up anguish and fury of the past few days raged through my body, and I dove right into Jason like a raging wildcat.

I hammered his body and face like there was no tomorrow. I fought out of control, and I wanted to beat the living daylights out of him.

Finally, I made a hammer of both fists together, and swung hard into his jaw. The fierceness of that blow lifted him up a mite, and then he slammed to the ground—unconscious.

I sat down; rather, I stumbled and fell down. I lay there for a few minutes gasping for breath. That guy was hard.

Finally, I dragged myself up to my feet and retrieved my gunbelt. I handcuffed Jason's hands behind his back, and then moved to the woman. She was unconscious, but alive.

I untied her, tenderly picked her up and carried her to the wagon. I lay her in the wagon bed, and then went back for Jason. He was coming to and struggling with the cuffs.

"Take these irons offen me and let's finish this," he growled at me.

"It is finished", I said. You are going to jail.

I grabbed him up and he lunged at me again with his whole body.

I had all I was going to take from the likes of him, and I slipped my Colt out and laid him a good one along the side of his head. He slumped to the ground—out like a lamp.

I exhaled. Well, only one way to take him back. I dragged his unconscious body to the edge of the ravine and rolled him down it.

Then, I casually walked down to the wagon. He was still out when I got there.

After I got him to his feet and lifted him to lay face down over one of the wagon horses, I lashed him there with a length of rope. There was no way that I wanted him in the bed of the wagon with Mrs. Moulter.

"O.K., Warrior, let's get back to Creede."

I climbed up into the wagon seat and set that team moving back toward Creede. Warrior trailed along behind the wagon.

It was some time later when we pulled up in front of the sheriff's office and jail. Sheriff Tulley and his boys stepped out to the plank boardwalk and looked at Jason.

"You both look like Hell, Cole, what happened"

"We tripped and fell," I said with a sarcastic grin spreading across my sore, cut, and swollen face, "Lock him up good, and watch him careful. The charge is attempted murder."

I drove the wagon with Mrs. Moulter back to the doctor's office, and waited while he checked her out. She would be all right, but she needed to stay with the doc and his wife for a few days. I checked on Toby as well, and he would be all right in a week or so. He would be quite sore during that time. Broken ribs do that. Allyson was with him, and he was in much better spirits. That was enough to make sure that he came through it.

Finally, I decided then that maybe I should ride back to the Lower Colorado. Something may have happened there, and they might have need of me. The thought hit me then, "I sure wish that Laura had need of me."

CHAPTER TWENTY-TWO

"The Stockton Memorial Service"

Word of the pending Stockton Memorial Service at the church passed quickly through the small town. Friends and mourners were there. Every business in town was closed except for a few saloons. Curious people were there. Even a few who feared him, hated him, and despised him were there.

It was around 2:45 in the afternoon when Laura Sumner, escorted by James Saunders entered the church building. They were followed by all of Laura's wranglers. Louise Montrose was already there.

Other mourners filed on in, and the streets of town appeared deserted. A few who despised Cole Stockton and the Law sat grinning in their favorite saloon—a drink in their hands. They would drink to Cole Stockton's entrance into Hell.

Sheriff J.C. Kincaid stood near the symbolic, but empty casket. He was frowning and staring hard at Saunders, who stared back with equal venom.

J.C. had it in the back of his mind to tell Laura all about Saunders, and then call him out. After all, he had nothing to lose but his life. It would, he thought, cause Laura to open her eyes and see James Saunders for what he was—a killer, one who would have shot Cole Stockton down, given the chance. It was the least he could do for his fallen friend.

Laura Sumner had thoughts, regrettable thoughts. If only she had not sent Cole away, he might still be alive. She wished that she could see him again. She would make it up to him. There was not even a body to take a last loving look at. A last look at his sunburned face would last her a lifetime. Now, it was all gone. Cole Stockton would be just a memory in time. Laura trembled with grief.

Louise Montrose sat hanky in hand with a few of her girls, her main bartender, and a couple of friends. She was visibly sorrowful. Her normally bright brown eyes were red-rimmed and misty. She watched J.C. Kincaid with thoughtful looks. She was a fool not to have seen it before. She wondered if J.C. would ever look at her with pining eyes again. She would speak to him after the services.

The Reverend George Daniels began the solemn service with a prayer for the recently departed soul of Cole Stockton.

* *

It was roughly about three o'clock when Warrior and I entered town and found it somewhat deserted except for a couple of saloons and the local church. By the number of horses and wagons lined up out front, it looked a lot like someone important had passed away. I spotted "Mickey" tied to one of the hitching posts and I swallowed hard.

"Maybe, I could just get a glimpse of Laura," I thought, and rode up beside Mickey. I dismounted and slowly walked to the door.

The church was crowded, so I just stood in back of the crowd. I looked over heads and shoulders trying to find Laura amongst the obvious mourners. I couldn't hear the Reverend as he spoke his praises and prayers, but I'm sure that the deceased, whoever it was, would appreciate them greatly.

Then, I saw J.C. Kincaid move to the front of the crowd and point his finger at someone in the front row. He sure looked like he was spouting some powerful words. Just then, a fancy dressed "gentleman" stood up, rather, jumped up and swept his coat back to reveal his hardware. What was happening?

Laura Sumner sprang to her feet and faced the fancy-dressed man. Her face looked stricken with surprise and anger. The fancy dressed dandy pushed her roughly away. Laura staggered back into the coffin, then slipped to the floor.

Anger overcame me, and I pushed through the crowd amongst some audible heavy gasps and wide-eyed stares. One elderly lady fainted.

The fancy dressed man sported two bone handled Colt .44's and I suddenly recognized him.

"Dandy Jim" Saunders was facing off with J.C. Kincaid in a room filled with bystanders.

There was no way that J.C. could even come close to Saunders in a gunfight. I forced my way to the forefront of the crowd as fast as I could.

Louise Montrose had jumped up also and she was headed toward J.C.

Suddenly, both men flashed for their weapons. I reached for my Colt at the same instant. There was no time to shout.

* *

Louise Montrose heard Kincaid accuse Saunders of coming to this town in order to kill Cole Stockton. She saw what was happening, and jumped up, moving toward J.C. She had just reached him and pushed up against him, right in the line of fire.

Saunders had drawn his weapon and was lining up that Colt straight at Kincaid. He was squeezing the trigger when a shot reverberated through the room.

A heavy .44 revolver slug took Dandy Jim Saunders squarely in the right hand, smashing all the bones and driving the just-firing pistol toward the back wall of church. The bullet smacked harmlessly into the wall.

J.C. Kincaid's revolver had just cleared leather. He was bringing his Colt to bear on Saunders when Louise Montrose falling into him suddenly threw him off balance. Both of them crashed to the floor. Luckily, his revolver never fired.

The entire crowd turned to face the newcomer. Standing at the front of the wide-eyed and disbelieving crowd was a dusty, sweaty, scratched up, and slightly swollen-faced U.S. Marshal Cole Stockton— alive. He held a smoking Colt Revolver in his hand.

James Saunders crouched holding his smashed and bleeding right hand—his favored gun hand. He would later discover that he could never use it again. His eyes were filled with pain and fear. Anyone else would have shot him again—to make sure that he was dead. He would've done it to Stockton. Why didn't the man shoot him again? He looked fearfully at Stockton.

U.S. Marshal Cole Stockton looked Dandy Jim Saunders straight in the eye and quietly ordered him out of town, out of the Lower Colorado, and advised him never to return, or pay the ultimate price— his life. James Saunders knew that he wouldn't return. Cole Stockton was a man of his word, and Saunders knew that Stockton would indeed kill him. He was going east, never to return to the West again. A couple of citizens drew their revolvers and escorted Dandy Jim Saunders to the doctor's office for treatment.

* *

Sheriff J.C. Kincaid stared incredulously into the softly tearing brown eyes of Louise Montrose.

"J.C., you could have been killed! What would I do if you weren't around for me?"

He was dumbfounded. Louise actually cared for him. He looked into her eyes with tenderness, and she smiled back at him.

"You big dumb goof. I LOVE you."

Louise Montrose pressed herself more firmly against J.C., and they kissed.

* *

Laura Sumner stared at Cole Stockton with widened eyes. She couldn't believe it. Was it a ghost? Her heart pounded as she slowly, at first, moved toward the tall slender figure. Her eyes misted over, and tears of joy formed streams that rolled down her cheeks. She ran to him, stopping just inches in front of him.

She looked up into his eyes and saw the tenderness that she remembered. His face was cut, scratched up, and a bit swollen. One eye looked darkened and puffy. His lower lip was cracked and split with dried blood. He looked as if he had been in an extremely violent fistfight. That seemed highly unlikely. Cole Stockton didn't partake of fistfights.

They searched each other's eyes for a long moment. Jud Ellison and the rest of the wranglers crowded around them. They could almost feel the magnetic undying passion that passed between Cole and Laura.

Cole held out a swollen left hand to Laura. She placed her soft hand in his and she felt the warmth that she had missed the past few days. She looked questioningly into his eyes and she saw the slightly sheepish grin begin to spread over his sunburned face.

She moved into his arms, laying her head against his shoulder. His left arm went around her waist pulling her into him. He touched her soft dark hair lightly with a bruised right hand. He held her close for a moment, and then she lifted her face to him. The kiss was long and warm. At last they parted and Laura again looked up into Cole's eyes.

"Let's go HOME, Cole."

"AMEN!" chorused a group of wranglers.

Printed in the United States
By Bookmasters